Wilbur Schmarr was born in South Africa much to the consternation of his mother who was forty at the time. After completing two engineering degrees, he worked for Siemens, then performed aerospace work in two countries. He retired after forty service years to live in South Africa with his wife and one son. He also has children in the UK and Australia.

Dedicated to my soul mate, Florence, I am so lucky to have found you.

Wilbur Schmarr

Master Builders

AUSTIN MACAULEY PUBLISHERS™

LONDON • CAMBRIDGE • NEW YORK • SHARJAH

A CIP catalogue record for this title is available from the British Library.

ISBN 9781398479791 (Paperback)
ISBN 9781398479807 (Hardback)
ISBN 9781398479821 (ePub e-book)
ISBN 9781398479814 (Audiobook)

www.austinmacauley.com

First Published 2022
Austin Macauley Publishers Ltd ®
1 Canada Square
Canary Wharf
London
E14 5AA

Thank you to all of the people that encouraged me along my writing path, especially those who helped with the English and those that made constructive manuscript content suggestions.

Table of Contents

Chapter One

(Where the Revelation Begins)

'So much for the kak[a] story about tunnels and bright lights,' thought Chris Petersen as he reacted to the sudden unpleasant jarring sensation that rattled his teeth. The sensation made him think of snapping out of being half asleep to being fully awake or even falling onto concrete after jumping out of the seventh storey of a building. Death was meant to be a relatively pleasant situation with relatives standing by while you investigated 'the light'. You were meant to experience a release from pain. One was meant to leave existence with a soppy grin on your face since you would soon see your ancestors around you, ancestors that would guide you through 'the valley'. They would help you with 'the judgement'!

At this time Chris could conclude 'no way'. This unpleasant re-arranging of one's bones was no fun. Unfortunately, there was no one to complain to as far as Chris could tell from the deathly silence. So, where was the traditionally promised help?

---

[a] This is a traditional South African manner of referring to human excrement. Ignore the term if expletives offend you.

Chris thought back to his demise. Realisation came that he had broken one of the electrical Ten Commandments[b]. So much for being a highly qualified and experienced electrical engineer! He had inadvertently grabbed hold of the high voltage terminal without thinking, the terminal unfortunately lacking earth leakage protection. The full force of the high voltage electrical energy had surged through his torso and locked his hand around the terminal in an unbreakable death grip. Heart fibrillation initiated rapidly and his clenched jaw and grating teeth blocked his feeble attempts to call for help. Light faded into darkness as his entire complement of hairs rose and blackened. The electrical energy resulted in a generally messy cooking process that terminated all bodily functions irrevocably. Chris shuddered at the memory. He did remember falling forward and that was it. Without even having been granted the time to let his life flash past him at the time, Chris waited hopefully for the bright light at the end of the tunnel to appear as promised. Disillusionment! Death had followed too quickly and the muscular spasms were too painful to allow coherent thought, other than the irrational hope that any light at the end of the tunnel was not a train. Chris opened his eyes.

'Just a minute, how can that be possible?' thought Chris. If you pegged you pegged and eyes were left behind for the worms. Yet here was the situation. Chris could see light. He could think! His memory appeared to be intact. A grey expanse stretched around and above him like a cocoon. A

---

[b] "Causeth thou the switch that supplieth large quantities of juice to be opened and thusly labeled such that thy life may be a long and happy one in this valley of tears."

single fuzzy soft white light glowed in the centre of the grey ceiling directly above him. Chris had the feeling that he was lying on a comfortably soft yet unyielding surface. The silence continued unperturbed. Chris decided to raise his right arm and to bring it into view.

Movement! A claw-like object hove into view and Chris inspected it curiously. He opened and closed his hand and watched fascinated as six mechanical attachments that looked like talons clenched and relaxed.

'This cannot be,' thought Chris and waved his hand from side to side. The talons obliged obediently. Chris decided to sit up and all of his exercises over the years must have helped him to do so in one fluid motion without needing to slide his legs to the side.

'Marvellous fitness level those 5BX[c] exercises result in' thought Chris and then immediately realised that was 'before'; before arriving at this place. He remembered a surprised reaction from his physiotherapist years ago when he could sit up from a prone position without aid and without using his arms in order to do so.

He looked down to realise that he was nude. The term 'nude' was a misnomer as he realised that there was no flesh, no hair and no genitalia to be seen. Chris screamed aloud on the discovery that the parts of his (body?) that could be seen were grey, unrecognisable, featureless and definitely not human. They seemed to be just as grey as the rest of this place. The realisation of the loss of gender was a hard knock. The

---

[c] The term 5BX denotes 'Five Basic Exercises' that take up to 12 minutes per day, a regimen adopted by the Canadian Armed Forces to raise the fitness level of the Canadian military population.

joke came to mind about losing the capability to think as a result of the unkindest cut of all. Screaming seemed to be therapeutic so Chris let loose a salvo of blockbusters that rocked the grey featureless ceiling.

'Ag[d] no man,' said a voice to Chris' left. 'There is no need to act like a schoolgirl.'

Shocked by the sudden intrusion to the silence, Chris jerked his head to the left and almost screamed again. An apparition that could only be from someplace like Mars greeted his sight. A smooth grey dome (was everything grey in this place?) pierced by four lenses with red centres (making him think of internet web cameras) greeted his gaze. Weird extensions to the side of the dome made Chris think of a mobile stereophonic surround-sound speaker system. Two arm extensions under the dome made Chris think of a robot in a science fiction novel.

'Alright then I understand,' stated the apparition. 'I also freaked out the time I met my mentor now that I think about it,' boomed the mechanical spectre.

'What, what, what,' spluttered Chris.

'Time enough for questions later,' boomed the voice. 'I have to run your system diagnostics to confirm your serviceability level so that we can get on with our job. Stick around while I shut you down temporarily.' A six-taloned appendage moved to the side of Chris' head and there was immediate oblivion.

---

[d] South Africans tend to use such terminology inclusive of others such as 'Ja nee' or 'Ja well no fine.' This helps them to feel macho and unique.

Chapter Two

(Where Chris Interacts with His New Mentor)

The realisation that there was light, but no sound, again penetrated Chris' brain. He carefully moved his head from side to side, viewed the now familiar grey ceiling with the fuzzy light and managed not to scream this time. A sudden 'click' indicated the presence of sound.

'Good' approved the voice. 'You check out OK so we can get on with it.'

'Get on with what and who the eff[e] are you?' Chris demanded in a shocked tone of voice. 'What have you done to me?' he agonised.

'I am your mentor Brian Philby and I have recruited you to the Sentient Species Test and Evaluation Program or SSTEP for short,' intoned the grey dome solemnly.

'This is a step towards madness alright,' observed Chris. 'I'm losing it for sure,' he thought. 'I am stark staring bonkers or I am dreaming.'

---

[e] Human beings (and others) tend to use expletives beginning with the letter 'F' that sometimes relates to procreation. If the concept is strange or offensive to you then please ignore this term.

'No, you are none of the two,' said Brian in a dry voice. 'And yes, I can communicate with you via sound or indirectly via our subliminal communications sub system. You need only think. The subliminal communication channels have been specially opened so you can communicate with me anytime and anywhere. Just please try to be selective what you burble about so you don't disturb my concentration.'

'You mean I now have a built-in radio transmitter?' burbled Chris. 'What happened to me?'

'Well, you made a right real mess of yourself back on Earth,' observed Brian. 'You turned most of your body into a piece of charcoal. The stench was something to experience from what I heard and saw on our remote sensors. The one paramedic was sick halfway through the clean-up process while helping the clean-up team. You know that burnt human flesh is quite poisonous to other homo sapiens and pongs like mad. If you like I can set up a scenario playback from our records. We recorded the whole thing for you using our test and surveillance insect remote sensors in case you wanted proof that going back to Earth was not possible for you.'

'So how the eff did I end up here and where is here?' whined Chris in a panic.

'There is no need to swear you know. We have monitored you for years, indeed decades. We have been downloading your knowledge and experience in digital form in an on-going fashion on the expectation that you would make a hash of it or die from natural causes sooner or later. Knowledge is just a bunch of electrical impulses coupled to an organic data store you know. We replicated your unique data quite easily by using the tap-offs provided by our specialised surveillance sensors and signal fourier analysis. We have loaded the

16

resulting database into a mechanical shell specially designed for you. Your database is mostly complete and the human foible of forgetfulness is a thing of the past. You have a vast built-in database that you can call upon at will and you can also tap into our central database. Just think that you no longer have the condition called 'Alzheimer's light' by some or 'A-Cubed-D-Squared'[f]! Gone are the days when age affects your memory. You might however notice that some of your memory is missing. Can you remember your primary school days?' asked Brian.

Chris pondered and came to the realisation he could remember snatches of secondary school and University but his primary school existence was lost. He started feeling indignant about it and was just getting into an enraged state when Brian interrupted his train of thought.

'Think of it this way. Several bad experiences where you were bullied unmercifully and the sickness in class episode have not been retained to clutter your memory. Think of it as selective memory oriented into a positive direction.'

'What sickness in class episode?' demanded Chris. 'The one morning you spewed up your breakfast oats porridge all over the little blue tables that they had in the primary school class in those days. It formed a large white lumpy puddle in the centre of the table and then it spread out and dripped off the sides. You were mortified. The experience taught you to think of others when you saw the reluctance by which the

---

[f] References to Alzheimer's indicate the Homo sapiens tendency to forget. Age Activated Attention Deficit Disorder or AAADD, is another way of describing the same thing but in a severe sense.

mess was cleaned up on your behalf by a labourer and the disruption the episode caused in class.'

'Who decided what I would remember and what I wouldn't remember? Was I being censored?' asked Chris in an attempt to change the subject after he shuddered at remembering his memory's painted picture.

'You decided a lot of that yourself. You often destroyed our remote recording sensors (enhanced insects) with your cans of insecticide or by using weapons such your hands and using dangerous objects such as fly swatters. Several remote recordings were lost as a result. We have a policy that recording normally commences from about the age of five and we also remove episodes that have high emotional value (for example painful or embarrassing memories). We know what is painful from recording the sensory impulses generated in the brain and also reviewing the video captured by our sensors.

You must understand that your new digital memory is more than several thousand terabytes in size but it is still limited. Your file space manager will delete unimportant older records automatically when your memory is near to full. You don't want to start off or end up with a lot of useless junk in your files. You only need the detail that contributes towards making you the unique individual that you are with your knowledge in order to do your job. So, I say again that all of your technical knowledge and associated experiences are OK except for some recordings that you personally elected to destroy either directly or indirectly and we cannot do anything about that.'

Chris looked at Brian unbelievingly and after a long pause Brian continued while the fact sank in that Chris was no longer human, in fact he sounded more like a robot the more he thought about it.

'I can see that you thought that when you died you would miraculously awaken with all of your memory intact and that you would be in a perfect physical state. That is not so easy due to the aging DNA intentionally hidden in the human genes plus normal bodily wear and tear. Humans are forgetting parts of their existence and their experiences all of the time and the process accelerates in later life. Alcohol and age are great brain cell reducers. If you die when you are eighty years old (and when you have Parkinson's disease say) then there is very little that can be used from your memory at the point of death that is of value. So, recordings have to take place all the time in parallel for selected individuals. Life experiences for these selected individuals are stored centrally at this facility and many other facilities similar to it.

Contrary to popular belief, the human body on your Earth loses all of its functions at the time of death. An analogy is when a power source that is energizing an electrical circuit is disconnected, the circuit stops operating. A human body is a complex electrical circuit that runs on electrical impulses. The only way to reanimate an individual is to make use of recordings that were made prior to that individual's demise and to place them into an environment where these impulses can then be reenergised and animated.

As for what you are doing here, you are to be my assistant. Welcome to integration centre SS23 and SSTEP!' concluded Brian triumphantly.

'Why me?' whispered Chris after a long-dumbfounded silence where his jaw would have been hanging open slackly

19

if he had one. 'Does everyone get this sort of treatment? You did say selected individuals.'

'Not everybody is selected. We only pick those people that we feel will make a contribution to SSTEP. Attitude, aptitude and potential are prime attributes that are taken into consideration. There are however other programs and facilities at other locations that do their own recording and they have different needs to ours. There is a wide spectrum of life recordings taking place all of the time in a clandestine manner. You were deemed to have the correct SSTEP profile, the correct CV and the correct attitude to help us meet our SS23 objectives on schedule.'

Brian continued after a pause while fixing Chris with several red piercing glances. 'In comparison there are always several turkeys on Earth that lead a destructive or non-creative existence and as a result we have no interest in them. Even some such turkeys have recourse to an afterlife however. The dark teams typically recruit the worst of that group of humans. We have no interest in the dark team activities meaning that we do not prevent them from diverting us from our sphere of activities other than to balance the mayhem that they cause at times. I assume that you realise that the worst that can happen to people on Earth is that their experiences are not recorded and that they simply vanish from existence when they cease to survive in human form,' said Brian with a flickering red glint in his quad optics that Chris took as some regret or possibly glee.

'As for why you have been selected, think about the SSTEP prime objective and how privileged you are to have been selected. I can see that you are wondering what the SS23 objectives are so let me elaborate. The SS23 team has been commissioned by the galactic council to test the SS23 sentient species prior to allowing this newly developed species to be fielded. This location where we are is their specially selected new planet. Every planet has varying environmental challenges and that demands unique designs. Suitable planets are chosen for seeding purposes from the many trillions of planets in the universe and are hard to come by.'

'What do I know about different planets and sentient species design?' quavered Chris.

'We don't primarily perform the design work; since that is the responsibility of the galactic council's design teams. We support him and his teams by doing the testing of the seeding produce that has been designed, as a part of the SS23 mandate as I explained earlier,' intoned Brian. 'You remember that you have been equipped to have access to a central database and your knowledge has been augmented with details that you could not have known about before your human death. As regards your experiences on your Earth, you have a good understanding of the generic system testing process and human genealogy, given your research on your family tree and your DNA testing initiatives. You understand what and how to test system functions if you are given a system specification. You might even participate in writing seeding specifications in future, which we can tailor or adapt to the topic of sentient species seeding in our universe. After all, you have been involved with the development of unmanned aerial vehicles for most of your life and you used to be a system engineer. The specification practices and the resulting tests associated with the process that you mastered are similar to what we do in SSTEP. This is very important to SSTEP bearing in mind that you tested systems that could operate totally independently and operate autonomously without outside interventions. Those UASs [g] of yours with their artificial intelligence that had to act independently, fit very nicely into what we have been commissioned to do here at SS23.'

'This destroys all of my beliefs in terms of what the afterlife was meant to be all about!' agonized Chris. 'What about the issue of Judgment?' he asked Brian fearfully.

'OK. I can see we are going to have to go through the twenty questions routine until you fully understand the new order of things around here. I respect that there are certain beliefs back on your Earth and you were programmed not to question them when your human sentient species was designed. Rules were programmed in place to prevent mayhem and establish some form of law and order. Regarding judgement I can arrange for a performance appraisal with the galactic council workgroup associated with that if you like. Remember what your own experiences were when you had subordinates reporting to you back on Earth, the process is similar here. You were meant to reach agreement up front with your supervisor regarding expected performance, to have a written contract as regards your behaviour, your outputs and the applicable measurement criteria. Then you would work and your supervisor would compare expected performance against contracted performance at regular appraisal times. Possibly, salary increments or bonuses resulted accordingly. Now consider this in your life's context. Did you have such an agreement or contract; did you have any say in what you

---

[g] Unmanned Autonomous System

were meant to do when you became self-aware as a human being?' queried Brian with a wry glint in his quad red optics.

'Were you aware of any regular appraisal? Were you sure of the rules? I can however assure you that there were regular appraisals in accordance with rules and that the appraisals took place against our generically accepted universal principles and values. You were programmed with those without your knowledge from birth. These rules are often different than many that were lauded as being acceptable on your Earth. What do you think the result of any final appraisal would be, given that we have already chosen you for SSTEP? Our acceptance means that you have automatically passed the entry criteria. You are loyal, dedicated, you like helping others, you are patient, meticulous and you are not destructive,' concluded Brian.

'What about the Ten Commandments?' burbled Chris. 'Aren't we meant to be judged against the quality of the life that we led?'

'It is true that the galactic council has many and varied rules that we all have to abide by. The chairperson tends to get pissed off by individuals and species that kill each other (after all of the effort put into establishing them in the first place) hence the ruling to not destroy creation. On the other hand, there have to be challenges otherwise species stagnate and do not progress. Wars are sometimes a necessary evil specially to regulate a seeding's birth rate. A species could proliferate to an extent that they run out of their planet's resources to sustain life before they can seed other planets. So that is why there are basic rules that the galactic council mandates in each species' Basic Programming or the BP[h] as we call it.' Brian paused and was silent for a time while fixing Chris with another quad piercing glance before continuing.

'There is the rule of self-determination that the galactic council is very sticky about. The performance of selected individuals in a seeded species is monitored during life for this reason and thus judgment occurs in real-time and not suddenly at demise. Further to this we have learnt that every species requires rules and legends to use as a crutch in the survival game. So, the only exception to the self-determination rule for us is to provide a simple set of rules for a species soon after their seeding in their own world. After that it is up to the species. We do not directly (visibly) interfere unless specifically allowed to do so by the galactic council or if we wish to recruit other species to SSTEP,' Brian reflected again before continuing.

'For the times that the self-determination rule was not applied properly we ended up with a species having no ambition or spark, a lot of lazy whiners expecting the master builders to do everything for them. No initiative and no innovation, no advancement. No pain, no gain.'

'What about this story of there being one Creator, a Creator that wiped out life with a great flood and then restored it via the ark, what about Adam and Eve?'

'The fact is that it takes a team of dedicated master builders to successfully design, tailor, test and seed a sentient

---

[h] Basic Programming relates to the core program or set of rules that runs in each sentient entity. In humans and most sentient species the most basic rule is the rule of survival that triggers the flight or fight reaction.

species onto a planet, to ensure that the sentient species survives, enjoys life and provides us builders with pleasure in the process. It takes hundreds, indeed thousands of builder team members to do an effective job. Each ecology has several sub-species that rely on each other. Each sub-seeding requires a team of seasoned designers and testers. We have healthy competition between teams, to yield deigns that vary from microbes to dinosaurs, there are galactic design reviews where competing designs are compared and credits are provided to the best teams and their designs. On your Earth, there were several design teams that won awards. The tyrannosaurus rex and platypus design teams are examples of teams that won awards. Each environment and its ecology are very delicate and interdependent. You should thus appreciate that we are primarily benevolent, believe you me. On the other hand, we have also had to learn things the hard way and we have made mistakes along the way. We had to use the best means at our disposal to ensure that a seeding succeeded and to rectify any misadventures that occurred. These days our sentient species seeding process success rate is improving but sometimes we have to act in a manner that might be considered to be harsh by some, such as deleting a seeding.'

'Just a minute! How can the destruction of a species or allowing natural disasters to take place like the flood be benevolent?' demanded Chris righteously.

'For simplicity's sake, the belief of a worldwide flood was propagated intentionally on Earth for reasons that are obvious to us as builders. Before we get onto the issue of one massive flood and the use of nuclear weapons to delete a failed seeding, let us discuss DNA and seedling design variance. You understand statistics, being an engineer. You also understand the basics of DNA. If you have one male and female and if they further procreate with their children as do their subsequent progeny then you end up with the results of incest, something that is not allowed in most cultures on Earth. Two heads or having deformed feet is an example of the results of in-breeding. Think about mongrel dogs. Did you notice that mixed breeds are hardier when it comes to resistance to diseases or that breeds from a gene pool that is sufficiently separated? All cases of a single sourced DNA pool with minimal DNA marker variations results in deformities and eventual species extinction. That cannot be negated fast enough by the built-in evolution function that is a part of all new seeding designs. The thought of only two individuals of each class and sub-class seeding a world is not practical. Put another way, we had many Adams and Eves on your Earth placed at several far-away locations from each other at once. We seed several variants of various combinations of DNA pools on one world at several different locations at the same time when we move into any seeding project implementation phase. This you must have realised from the fact that several languages surfaced in many places at once on Earth, that different physical traits and languages exist and that groups eventually came into contact with each other and have inter-married,' Brian intoned before continuing.

'The basic human capability of speech was pre-programmed but the resulting languages are as diverse as the multitude of locations that were seeded on Earth. Many hundreds of locations were chosen with thousands of subtle DNA variances. These allow eventual intermingling and gene pool strengthening to operate in parallel with genetic mutation and evolution. This does not only apply to human beings; it applies to the entire ecology and life support system. Billions of variables and entities apply. So, physically speaking it is impossible to put all of the required DNA samples onto one ship in uncompressed form. Compression of the data in digital form is mandatory for practical reasons. Having a single ship such as your mythical ark that is big enough to guarantee species survival is not practical, but is a useful legend for species to believe in, until they 'come of age' and can be accepted into the galactic empire without trying to kill off all other sentient species. Tolerance has to grow with time. So, we establish blueprints in digital form by using our Tri-D memory cube technology. Several Tri-D cubes have to be deployed at several locations in parallel. Then the seeding progresses based upon the blueprints in the cubes. Accounts of your ark were oversimplified; we maintain the required database for re-implementation of the seeding in digitally modified form if it is necessary to terminate an unfortunate seeding. The compressed version of the design typically just fits onto one Tri-D memory cube. We tailor a seeding to a particular planet and introduce corrective measures for the next attempt with a new cube build release, if necessary, to better the chances of success next time in case of failure,' Brian explained. 'We are also experimenting with new techniques in SS23 that are less prone to needing these many gene pools but this has proved to be very difficult', again Brian paused.

'Further to this flood thing do the sums. The issue being that rain took place for forty days and forty nights all over the Earth at once? That water had to come from somewhere. Let's assume we stole it from Mars using huge space ships, so we had enough. Let's not waste time assuming that we used precious Higgs Bosons[i] to create the giga tons of water required for now. Let us conservatively assume that twenty millimetres fell in one hour. For now, assume a flat earth and that the earth does not soak up a lot of the water. Multiply the rainfall by twenty-four hours in the day and then by forty days. This results in 19200 mm or 192 metres. If your Earth were not flat, for people in Johannesburg that are at an altitude of say 1500 metres above sea level, the impact would be relatively minor. A sustained rainfall ten times as heavy would be required to make a real impact to people that are high up and rainfall that heavy would be certain to founder any ship inclusive of any ark (and the size of the vessel would have to be a lot larger than the Titanic, shall we say a million times larger to be able to sustain all of the creation species on Earth)? There is actually no record of a protective force field being applied to any arc on Earth to prevent her foundering in our seeding records. We also have the prime directive mandating no direct interference in the seeding's progression via pre-programmed evolution once the seeding has been validated.' Only a failed seeding has mandated eradication and interference to date and that requires approval at the highest levels,' said Brian with a wry glint in his optics before starting off again.

'For people at sea level the impact of the metres (or many metres) of rain per hour would be another matter compared to

---

[i] The Higgs Boson was being sought in the Large Hadron Collider particle accelerator facility located close to Geneva in 2012 and thereafter with some success. The 'God Particle' was claimed to generate mass, the mass that old Earth humans are all made of.

the effect at sea. Let us also consider the potential catastrophic effect of all of the world's volcanoes being suddenly submerged in water. Remember Krakatoa? Steam explosions can be very messy. We don't want to crack a planet in half with a steam explosion, or hundreds of them, do we? Alternatively, lots of Tsunamis from the explosions would destroy all of the millions of food sources on land that we so laboriously put in place. Each world has its own (limited) supply of water and food. It takes time to grow crops from seeds. To add to the allocated quantity of water on any planet requires immense amounts of energy, an exercise that can affect the stability of the planet's orbit due to the mass of water involved,' said Brian waving his mechanical arms around for emphasis.

'An earthquake can shorten the length of the day by a few microseconds so think of the effect of suddenly adding a few billion tons of water to the orbit of any planet around the sun. The Sun pulls at the Earth with a force proportional to the masses of the two celestial bodies. If the Earth's mass were to be suddenly increased significantly this would affect the Earth's orbit and could cause the Earth to move closer to the Sun. This would increase the surface temperature and could start boiling all of that water. Small changes have immense consequences on a planet. By just tilting the Earth's axis slightly and moving the Earth further versus closer to the Sun we established the desired patterns of summer and winter to sustain the complex ecological seeding on Earth. A global flood would have destroyed an immense amount of work performed by the master builders relating to the Earth's seeding where you originated. That would have required the seeding work to be repeated, so we normally avoid such drastic measures. We do however intentionally propagate urban legends, myths and beliefs that help to keep a seeding moving on and coming of age.'

Chris was suitably cowed and could not find anything to say, not even to burble about a little.

'It was tough finding a suitable moon so that there would be light at night and then to introduce the moon into Earth's orbit from afar without causing too many earthquakes and floods. You poor Earthlings at the time were so scared of the dark and still had to learn about fire when that intervention of providing a night-light for them took place,' said Brian dryly.

'Now consider the aftermath of the flood. Where did all of the water go? Sucked up by the volcanoes? Sent back to Mars? Your spaceship Earth is a closed environment that has to obey the laws of the creation, conservation of energy and the creation or destruction of matter. The closed environment rule that applies to Earth doesn't easily allow for the additional creation of mass from energy or vice versa. The reverse process of creating energy from mass is violent and extremely destructive. It all relates to the energy available to the builders and that is constrained. Looking up at the sky at night you must have realised that there are many trillions of billions of stars and planets. To put them there took a lot of energy. To modify each one significantly to suit silly foibles for each of the seedling inhabitants of each specifically chosen planet is an unaffordable luxury,' concluded Brian dryly. 'Putting your Moon where it is, was hard enough work'.

'The legend and circumstantial evidence of a massive flood had to be established however to introduce a healthy level of fear in the human species (to help reduce the potential for chaos by maintaining some semblance of law and order). We just funnelled a lot of heated seawater in the form of rain into a relatively small area surrounded by a relatively small force field close to sea level. The perception resulted that the whole world had been flooded and that everybody had better behave themselves in future! We could do that without disturbing the planet too drastically and involved temporarily moving sea water, not by creating any more water. Embellishments and exaggerations over time resulting from the intervention yielded the required seeding level of respect expected by the master builders and the galactic council. This applies especially for a seedling sentient species that lacks the technology and understanding in those days relative to what it might have today,' said Brian quietly.

'You still seem to be sceptical about the concept of benevolence,' he said glancing at Chris. 'Remember once again that it takes incredible dedication, a lot of work and a lot of energy to establish and seed a sentient species given an interdependent ecology. We have every desire to see the species survive, grow and enjoy life and the success of that is our reward. We build-in some protective interlocks in every species' BP to prevent them from destroying each other up to a point and we have many such species in the cosmos. We are determining an optimised species design using an on-going process. A lot of your inherent capabilities in the seeding on Earth were intentionally suppressed. This was to prevent you from killing each other from afar by using teleportation or telekinesis for example,' explained Brian.

'The BP is actually quite complex and varies between the sexes. Men have this inquisitive experimental streak in them that often gets them into trouble with nature. Most men of your Earth have to provide for their family and as such were designed to be protective of their mate and the union's children. Most women are basically programmed to be the family caretakers and to ensure the safety of the offspring. Without women, men tended to work themselves to death since the pre-programmed drive to solve technical problems meant that food was not important. Woman have an innate programmed BP rule to get their men to eat. Both sexes have very strong needs for ensuring the procreation of the species and the survival of the family unit but the BP allows for individual choices. Some seedlings lead more exemplary lives than others,' intoned Brian.

'We have made mistakes in the past where we had to intervene in a final manner in order to rectify the situation and this distressed us greatly. Your primary efforts will be directed towards preventing that unacceptable situation from happening again,' Brian said quietly.

'What do you mean when you talk about a final manner?' asked Chris curiously.

'We have had to detonate nuclear warheads on Earth to cauterize a colony of human misfits that had begun to multiply out of control due to genetic manipulation and their intention to decimate the rest of the population. An urban legend was created of people being turned into 'pillars of salt' as a result. Pillars of carbon are closer to the truth.'

Chris contemplated the implications of what Brian had said. His thoughts were interrupted when Brian continued sombrely.

'If you have a species malfunction rate of one in a thousand and you have a population of several billion individual seedlings then you could have millions of unacceptable mutations. Your job will be to test many such combinations and scenarios in the SS23 facility. You will perform so-called 'Monte Carlo'[j] simulations and many of those. You will have to perform these design variant simulations in order to test the seeding before it is deployed on a designated new planet, to ensure that the probabilities of success are acceptably high, that is within an acceptable probability spread. On Earth you were taught about the concept of six sigma. These days we demand a process success probability even higher than that. We did however also capitalise on the nuclear warhead cauterisation event by telling the remaining population to lead an exemplary life. Fear of retribution is a powerful motivator. Unfortunately, we did leave some evidence of the nuclear explosion on your Earth, as evidenced by rocks being vitrified, a hard-smooth glasslike state.'

'What about the, uh, rewards for leading an exemplary life in my case?' asked Chris timorously.

'Ag no man. Now we are back to ground that I thought we had covered. Think about the concept and apply your logic. Do you really think that you were going to sit around on clouds strumming a harp out here after you left your existence on Earth? Did you believe that we have free knock shops on every corner interspersed with bars giving away drinks for free that never close and with no babalas[k] as a consequence the next day? What did you really enjoy doing on Earth?'

---

[j] Monte Carlo simulations involve varying multiple process input variables to ascertain what each variation results in as an output from the process.

[k] South Africans refer to a hangover as a 'babalas'.

There was a silence that stretched out for some time before Chris could marshal his thoughts.

'Well, I enjoyed challenges, building things, fixing problems and designing systems,' said Chris finally.

'So, doing something else or doing nothing is likely to bore you stupid isn't it? You are a workaholic and you are happiest when you are doing something creative, even if you have to do that for a long time? You remember how bored you used to get on holidays after a few weeks?'

'Well yes,' agreed Chris.

'Now you know why I recruited you to SSTEP,' boomed Brian forcefully, moving forward to accentuate the point. 'You are classed as an "A"[1] type person and you get a kick out of fixing things and designing new things. Doing anything else especially nothing is likely to be a severe punishment for you. Hence you are in your concept of Heaven right now, aren't you?'

'Well, I don't know. When I speculated about the afterlife, I felt I actually wanted to travel a bit you know, in particular visit other planets in the blink of an eye, that sort of thing. Not have to worry about work or responsibilities,' moaned Brian.

'You are likely to get tired of doing that after a while especially if you do it for millennia. Think again what happened when you went on holidays, that sense of boredom after a few weeks especially when the Mr Fix-it tasks were over and done with at your home. You lost your sense of meaning. A lot of us however do feel like you do as regards visiting the cosmos and as a result, we do travel a lot both for SSTEP and during our recreational periods,' smiled Brian.

---

[1] 'A' type people are workaholics and tend to be introverts.

'Smiled?' thought Chris. There was no evidence of any humour to be seen in the bland grey dome with its quadruple piercing red glance. Yet the warmth came through.

'You will get used to the way the subliminal communication channels work in due course,' quipped Brian. 'After a while it gets to be second nature.'

'If you say so,' said Chris doubtfully since he felt uncomfortable with having his innermost thoughts being read so easily. A sudden thought struck him. 'Tell me what the heck you did to my Willie!' he demanded indignantly.

'Your Willie was also somewhat decimated and parboiled in the fire that resulted from your nylon clothes busting into flame when you decided to waltz around clutching that live electrical connection back on Earth. A permanent erection in a shrivelled, black, fragile and non-feeling condition is not conducive to procreation or to peeing. Seeing as most humans are normally only issued with one Willie at a time, the Willie you had at your disposal was no longer functional; you can trust me on this. In any case you are now at a new build standard[m] meaning you have been upgraded relative to what you were on your Earth. You don't need a Willie.'

'What do you mean?' burbled Chris.

'Think back to Earth's physical records. People were a lot shorter in days gone by than they are now. Take the example of the suits of armour that used to be worn in the dark ages. The suits were tiny! It is strange that most of you human beings (other than those that are now part of SSTEP and who

---

[m] A Build Standard defines the design for a particular piece of equipment or species. A species of Ape is one build standard, Humans another and Master Builders yet another.

as a consequence fully understand the theory of evolution) normally cannot comprehend the concept of built-in evolution. Humans have been getting taller over the years in response to Earth's environmental challenges and that is only one of the proofs of the existence of the evolution capability that is programmed-in to each seeding design. This is the expected response that we built into your human BP. Mental capabilities are increasing and there is less mumbo jumbo or burning witches at the stake due to the self-modifying evolutionary master design that has been made part of every sentient species. The Homo sapiens build standard, the original design, the BP and all of the supporting ecology was established with the capability of adapting to its environment and it has been doing so for a long time. All species on your Earth must either evolve to survive or they will become extinct. The BP programming defines the core or basic sentient species evolution capability. Successful human beings and all of nature on your Earth have been evolving with time and exactly as they were designed to do,' said Brian.

'You are however more fortunate than most of mankind. You are now more capable than you were when you were on your Earth. In fact, you are more capable than the normal evolutionary process time-line would have provided you with. This holds true for even the next ten thousand evolutionary years on Earth. You have jumped your evolutionary queue. This is relative to dying from natural causes or mishaps such as charcoaling yourself. You could have evolved along with the rest of the Homo sapiens design for another ten thousand years before arriving at your currently improved state. Your new build standard is far advanced in comparison to what you

36

were. Your miniature nuclear reactor, your dark energy[n] harvester provides you with all of the power that you need. You don't need to eat. You need not handle any nasty smelling by-products of the digestive process either and your advanced fusion reactor products are benign. I say again, you don't need a willie.'

'Hey!' exclaimed Chris. 'Eating was one of my favourite pastimes! Never mind the drinking beer and wine part. The worst thought of all is missing out on sex.'

'There are capabilities built into your build standard that more than compensate for your perceived losses inclusive of sex if you just wait and see,' said Brian irritably. 'Even sex has been catered for at SSTEP.'

'Sorry,' said Chris guiltily with a sense of needing to learn a lot in this new environment and now not wanting to appear ungrateful.

'You will no longer experience pain as you knew it. There are however a few disadvantages. You will have to endure irritating automatic audio alarms when you over-extend your new form beyond its design limits and there are still some protective interlocks in your new BP to prevent you from damaging yourself. This is inclusive of a reasonable anti-suicide program, but even there you might have a choice. At least you won't be totally incapacitated if you experience an unplanned mishap as a result of the interlock feature in your BP. Your outer protective covering is strong and durable and

---

[n] Humans were still looking at ways of harvesting an energy source that they called 'dark energy' since it was not understood. Some humans believed that the Higgs Boson might theoretically operate on dark energy to create matter.

it can endure toxic atmospheres for when you perform sentient species seedling field-testing. Your improved 'hands' now include specialised tools that you can use to test, cut, extract, analyse and manipulate specimens. You have a mass spectrometer and laser cutter integrated into one arm. The other arm includes three-dimensional ultrasound, a heater and vibration inducing equipment.'

'A vibrator?' questioned Chris with a laugh and received a dirty look from Brian as a reward before Brian continued.

'Not that type of vibrator! You can perform environmental stress screening on your specimens, meaning that you can test them under temperature and vibration stresses. In addition to your mechanical agitator, you have the capability to warp into meta space and you can travel vast distances in microseconds if you tap into the Universe's dark energy or another energy source such as a nearby star. You can now fulfil that dream of yours to visit stars and planets in the cosmos at will. Just remember to log your visits with the traffic controller at central and also ensure that you have enough off-time leave credit so we can find you when we need you,' said Brian sternly.

'You still need to partake in the equivalent of sleep or to rest your logic circuits and to run detailed diagnostic tests; the consequences of rest deprivation are still madness or paranoia. Maybe in our build standard terminology 'central processor malfunction' is a better term.'

Chris went into burble overdrive and started shaking his head from side-to-side. Panic was starting to rear its ugly head again. 'This is impossible,' he muttered.

'Look Chris, you are going to have to snap out of this. Get a grip on yourself. Maybe now you can understand why there

38

have to be over-simplifications, legends and cryptic rules in place during the species seedling deployment phase on a new planet,' stated Brian grimly. 'If we do not simplify creation, especially for older seeding designs that have not evolved far enough to understand technology in general and the possibility of a different order of things, the seedlings display disbelief, total awe, depression, madness and self-termination tendencies. We had to build in an element of eternal hope and blind trust into each species' BP in order to ensure viability and acceptance of living conditions, conditions that might be very unpleasant at times.'

'Blind trust?' queried Chris.

'Yes,' responded Brian. 'Logical processes too. Remember your own experiences as a system engineer. You had to perform design reviews in order to verify system specifications and to achieve the best result. You had to do rapid prototyping. You had to test the design. Many minds working together results in a superior and coherent design. Remember that new species require legends and beliefs in order to initially exist in a significant manner. Remember that in relation to your observations of your life on Earth. Blind trust was one of the basic programming features that we had to build into the BP along with the automatic breathing and heartbeat sustaining programmes. Playing the Lotto works on blind trust as well as hope. Sentient species tend to be lazy since it is also so that gravity is daunting and unrelenting, so we had to enforce automatic functions at the lowest level of existence in the BP. Otherwise the species just stops breathing, digesting food or pumping its nutrients and fluids such as blood around. Let us talk about blind trust or faith some more,' suggested Brian.

'Let me give you an example. You believed that story about the British soldiers feeding the Boer women and children ground glass in the concentration camps during the Boer War in an attempt to kill them off, didn't you?' queried Brian.

'Well, yes,' answered Chris surprised that Brian knew so much about him and the South African situation on his Earth in particular.

'Let's explore that possibility by using simple logic. Let us assume that there are lots and lots of panes of glass available in the middle of a war and that you have soldiers being commanded to sit around and pound this glass into little pieces. The noise involved is one thing and the potential cuts involved something else, never mind the enemy bullets whizzing past while the pounding is going on. Let's investigate the real risk to human health. Do you remember that idiot of a Major in the Air Force that regularly got so drunk that he used to eat wine glasses as a party trick? Do you remember whom I mean, he used to lie in the ambulance you had at your test site the morning after an evening's party with an oxygen mask on his face? He believed that pure oxygen would reduce the effect of his babalas° and that eating glass was fun?'

'Well, yes,' said Chris in a subdued tone of voice.

'He survived you. He is also not alone as regards people munching on glass without apparent effect. Lots of clowns, idiots or party trick exhibitionists on old Earth try to prove how clever and unique they are by eating glass or other artefacts such as steel nails. They have this need to impress

---

° A babalas is still the South African term for a hangover.

others. Actually, it is true that there is a need to be appreciated and accepted by others that was built into the human species BP. This was to prevent a whole species of introverts or hermits living alone since swarms of introverts or hermits result in no procreation. Chewing nails might be one way to obtain the money to buy food to eat, so there is a resulting rationale as explained by Maslow's hierarchy[p].

The point being that glass is inert and is normally passed relatively harmlessly out of the gut without damage especially if there are no pieces with too many sharp protrusions. Small (relatively blunt) pieces are particularly innocuous. To survive the party trick, the smaller the pieces and the less sharp protrusions are, the better. Now, let us envisage a woman sitting in a concentration camp. Let's pretend it is your wife. What would she do if she detected hard pieces of whatever in the food, be it sand or glass?' queried Brian.

'Knowing her she would spit it out, yell like a stuck pig and look for a cook to beat to death' answered Chris in a timid tone of voice.

'Exactly,' said Brian. 'The idea of forcing people to eat small pieces of glass in the hope that it will kill them slowly is therefore preposterous. Induced starvation, sickness and lack of medical attention are much more potent when it comes to genocide. The environment on your Earth abounds with urban legends and misinformation. This brings me back to the point. We have had to program a certain acceptance, call it gullibility or innocence if you like, into each species' BP in order to reduce madness or self-extinction tendencies. We

---

[p] Maslow's hierarchy explains that you have got to eat, crap and pee before you do anything else.

originally believed we should act as paternal fathers and support a new species directly and visibly shortly after planetary seeding. Invariably that backfired on us; it resulted in weird and unhealthy customs. As an example, consider the braais[q] that we enjoyed so much on your Earth. Do they ring a bell?' asked Brian.

'Of course,' said Chris noting that Brian said 'we' and that Brian knew an awful lot about South African customs. He made a mental note to find out more about Brian's history in due course. A possibility existed of South African influences being at work here, or maybe Brian was a version of a previous colleague?'

'Well, we invited the leader of a group of a newly established species on Earth to a braai. We thought we were helping to establish a custom and to help the species to have fun and to appreciate what they had been given. The next we saw was these guys cremating meat inclusive of their own offspring on altars in some cases in the mistaken belief that they were honouring us. This is one of the reasons why the self-determination rule was put in place. We have to mostly maintain a low profile and let the pre-programmed evolution process in the BP take its course. We have to avoid being seen as 'Gods'. We are merely designers, testers and builders of new species.

Here is another example of the dilemma that we face in terms of how a seeded sentient species can miss the boat. We saw several individuals hobbling around with symptoms that could only be gout. Now, gout has various triggers and

---

[q] A braai is often termed a 'barbeque' in cultures other than the South African culture.

depends on the physiology of the individuals involved but we were able to identify a common cause for this specific group of people and that was over-eating pork. We suggested that alternative foods be considered and the next thing the issue became an edict with dire consequences if anyone ate pork.

'As a result, we had to make a lot of tough decisions. The decision to add certain gullibility to the species BP had to follow as regards establishing initial legends and to then let nature and eventually common sense take its course. Some individuals unfortunately exploited this generic gullibility. The Nazi propaganda minister in Germany exploited this human trait with extremely negative effects as seen during your Second World War. We were ultimately forced to let any species learn the hard way. You cannot warn a child to leave a heater alone until the child has experienced the pain from a burn and only then do you obtain belief and credibility. All species must learn the hard way and are then granted greater powers mostly by automatic evolution when they are more mature and less prone to ignore the rights of seeded species or to want to beat each other to death,' Brian solemnised.

'We came to realise that a species needs beliefs, legends and an awe of creation so we had to perform a little public dead seedling 'resurrection' in several places. We re-animated selected individuals that had different cultures and that had been publicly executed at various locations; so as to bring the respective seedlings witnessing the event into a state of awe. Technology sleight of hand but no magic! All we did was to repair the damage to the seedling bodies and then restore their mental state as it was recorded, at just before the time of death. This reanimation made the men and women public icons and reinforced fears as regards the builder capabilities, engendering adherence to social norms. Seedlings require public icons that tie them to the grand order of things otherwise they tend to get depressed and mayhem results. Luckily, the populace at the time did not monitor the mass of the men as they died and were reanimated. The slight mass loss and regain due to the installation of the digital technology would have been detected and the credibility of the demonstration might have been negated,' said Brian thankfully.

'Wow,' gasped Chris. 'I never realised how complex creation is and to what lengths master builders have to go.'

'You were not expected to fully understand creation as young sentient species seedlings hence our intentional simplification process. Remember that the self-determination rule mandates that we may not interfere with a species directly after seeding (except as a last resort and only with permission) as regards the difficulties they experience. It is a fact that only when a species works hard at something is anything that is done valued. Some humans understand this in their interactions with wild animals. The saying "Let Nature takes its course" means "Give evolution the time to do its job".'

'You have been fitted with some hardware interlocks to help you to comply with the prime directives since it is more difficult to comply with these directives than you might think and even you will have difficult choices to make,' said Brian flatly. 'When you see a drowning child or monitor a known felon or dictator that is going to kill others it is difficult not to become a straw to clutch at or to act as an executioner and eradicate the threat. The future has too many alternatives or possibilities. By intervening you invariably make matters worse. Scientists on Earth also recognised the same thing.

44

They do not normally intervene when a lion kills a special cheetah that has been fitted with a radio collar. An exception is sometimes made in the case of the builders, if we have invested heavily in a particular individual and recording has begun. It is easier to obtain permission to intervene for such a case. We did so twice in your particular case.'

'You did? When?' asked Chris with an incredulous glint in his optics.

'The first time was at a time you were given a motorbike by your father. There was the day that you were driving the motorbike downhill at a speed that was not very wise, close to the sports ground close to where you lived. A curve in the road loomed and you started braking sharply with the front brake with the result that the front wheel steering started oscillating and vibrating badly. The prediction was that you were going to lose control, summersault over the curb and break your neck when the results of gravity manifested themselves. We intervened without you knowing it by applying unseen damping forces to the steering and the steering oscillations died away. You could make the turn in safety while also suddenly remembering to use the rear brakes. To give you credit at least you learnt to drive downhill more carefully from that point in time. We wanted you to remain on Earth a bit longer, to achieve your system integration and test experience predicted for your later life.'

Chris stared at Brian, speechless once again.

'Then there was the time that you almost drowned in your friend's swimming pool. That was actually a dark team assassination attempt that we countered. You couldn't swim properly yet and a so-called friend was temporarily influenced by the dark team. He pushed you in intentionally. He ran off to hide his treachery and no one realised that you were in difficulty. Shouting under water has never been very successful. When humans pop up out of water they tend to want to breathe instead of shouting. We helped you to plan the course of action of jumping up and down by pushing against the pool's bottom so you could breathe intermittently and migrate to the shallow end of the sloping pool where you could stand. In this case, it was easier to intervene since the dark teams attacked you and we could counter the attack to maintain a proper balance of forces.'

'Thanks,' said Chris quietly after a time and then raised a concern. 'So why didn't you prevent that bus disaster where many school children were killed after the bus ended up in that dam in South Africa next to the road after the driver lost control?' asked Chris.

'We didn't have anyone in the bus that was being recorded at the time and we cannot intervene all of the time, we have enough work to do as it is. Seedlings tend to propagate into the billions and we just don't have the manpower to monitor each individual. We want every sentient species to learn from its own mistakes such as ensuring the placement of proper road barriers and maintaining their own locally designed mechanical contraptions. We have limited resources and to keep helping people that persist in living next to volcanoes or insist on living on tectonic plate fault lines for example, does not make sense and it spoils them if we do intervene,' concluded Brian.

'Let us now discuss your part in the new order and your new capabilities and responsibilities. To allow you to comply with the self-determination prime directive you have been fitted with a cloaking device. You are able to render yourself invisible to any species under test at will. Certain situations will even trigger the cloaking device automatically. Just keep away from the satellites and aircraft on Earth and any other inhabited planet when you are cloaked. Your strong electromagnetic cloaking field messes up the Earth's Global Positioning System satellites and we don't want to cause disasters by boats and planes veering off course. Note that the same magnetic field causes the relatively delicate electronic microcontrollers in aircraft avionics to malfunction or even reset. It is not a pretty sight if the computers and navigation systems that the aircraft rely on to stay in the air, re-boot in the air,' stated Brian, confirming Chris' own experiences with aircraft avionics malfunctions and their catastrophic failure consequences.

'You asked about natural disasters and why the master builders cannot intervene in more than ninety-nine percent of cases. Let us discuss the balance that there has to be in nature, the issue of free choice versus BP pre-programmed responses or the option of molly-coddling seedlings,' philosophised Brian.

'Natural disasters and sickness will occur at random in any environment and must occur to challenge every species. Whose fault is it if the sentient species decides to build houses on a known earthquake fault line? The seedlings have free choice and you cannot tell me that the people in Los Angeles don't know that they live on a fault line. Neither tell me that the Texans don't know that there is a cyclone every three days in Texas on average. Yet they remain in those dangerous areas. In many cases those seedlings that escape these environmental challenges do so through dumb luck and statistical chance since we mostly do not intervene. That is the

47

way of things and it results in strong evolution tendencies in conjunction with innovative self-protective measures. Species do learn once they have evolved far enough and they come to understand the consequences of choice. Intelligence is the most powerful capability of all,' confirmed Brian.

'The blind trust built into the BP does unfortunately also result in a lot of urban legends and foolish irrational actions. We have seen that as a species evolves the true facts of their situation finally surface and irrefutable evidence negates or explains original beliefs. On your Earth there are now very few people that believe the Earth is flat especially after the Google Earth program using satellite images appeared on the Internet. There are however many people that enjoy preying on others by starting rumours since that gives them a feeling of superiority. Consider some examples of what is currently happening on your Earth. Take the example of chain-letter type viruses that are voluntarily spread by people that believe that something bad will happen to them if they break the chain. How can anyone on Earth monitor if or when a chain letter chain has been broken and how can the mundane transmission of data over a communication link result in prosperity? Seedlings have to learn the hard way to not take things at face value and to research what they are told. Once they do that sustainably then they surpass their basic programming and become worthy of further evolution,' said Brian soberly.

'I still have a problem with this concept of benevolence,' said Chris hotly. 'What about diseases, why there are diseases and how is it possible that these are allowed to blight progress,' asked Chris petulantly?

48

'To prevent species breeding out of all control we had to install natural population growth inhibitors such as sickness and predation. One species in the chain is food for the next link and that is part of the seeding.' Brian ignored the stunned, yet dawning understanding looks he was getting from Chris.

'It is true that there are the spoilers; the dark teams do things out of pure spite and malice. Do you remember those days during your childhood when you used to build tree houses?' asked Brian.

'Of course,' responded Brian.

'You remember that tree house in the willow tree next to the stream, the one with the foefie[r] slide and its system of pulleys, the walls, the roof and that innovative door lock of yours under the tree fork that was holding up the floor of the tree house?'

'I was very proud of that tree house design,' said Chris enthusiastically.

'You remember that vandals trashed all of your hard work, they cut the foefie wire and they also cut the nylon rope into little pieces, the rope you used to pull people up into the tree house via the slide?'

'That nastiness and spite still make me very angry,' growled Chris.

'Then you understand what drives the dark teams since they experience pleasure from being spiteful. They have full freedom of choice and sometimes the line between dark

---

[r] A foefie slide consists of a steel wire anchored at both ends, the ends being at different heights. A steel pipe is placed over the wire and an exciting gravity driven ride follows if one holds onto the pipe sliding over the wire. Another term for this is using a "zip line".

49

actions and what we have to do to ensure species' long-term survival and conformance to establish order becomes grey. The galactic council feels strongly about certain acts that are considered unacceptable and as a result there are hidden triggers resulting from automatic sensor monitoring. If a species performs a forbidden act, then the triggers are activated and typically result in unpleasant consequences such as AIDS and HIV. We will talk about that and the need to intervene or not in wars and natural disasters again in due course.'

'While you mention that, why are there so many wars?' asked Chris, 'Could you not have prevented or at least reduced those despite the non-intervention rule?'

'You still don't understand. The whole intervention issue is a matter of balance since wars are extremely destructive, yet they promote species advancement and they do teach terrible lessons,' stated Brian grimly.

'A pacifist tends to not be as innovative or driven like a person that is curious or is seeking revenge. We had to build in all of the emotions in your Earth's human seeding inclusive of aggression and we tried to balance that with compassion and love. Otherwise, one ends up with a species that sits around looking at each other and then no evolution takes place,' said Brian in a slightly bored tone of voice. Then he shifted in his seat and Chris could tell that he wished to move on.

'Enough. So much for your first twenty questions and my responses to those for today. I hope I have touched on most of the traditional frequently asked questions that arise when a new recruit is reanimated in SS23. We will continue with your

50

primary briefing in between your induction training and when we have time,' declared Brian.

'Now let us discuss your specific directive so you know what to expect at a high level. You are going to have to especially second-guess and test for the negative reactions that could result from the latest well-meant BP programming for the species that we are working on in SS23. You have to properly test SS23 seedlings, you need to design and implement test equipment and I will explain what that means in due course. Regarding our newest build standard species model, you are expected to formally report all strange behaviours that diverge from what we are prepared to accept according to our value system as regards the SS23 seedling laid-down specifications.'

'What do you mean, what must I do exactly?' burbled Chris with a sudden note of panic in his voice since this sounded very far away from any experience Brian had ever experienced.

'Your immediate task is to generate the Test and Evaluation Mater Plan, the TEMP for the SS23 build standard. I have told you that this system integration and test facility is dedicated to the evolution and test of the SS23 build standard. We want to seed this planet with the SS23 strain in around five of old Earth years,' stated Brian grimly.

'Of course, we will set up your full job description with defined outputs against the five-year schedule as soon as you accept your job in principle.'

Chris floundered around with the strange concepts that he had been exposed to washing through his newly crafted brain and he could not think of anything to say.

'Tell me when you have snapped out of it,' said Brian caustically after a lengthy uncomfortable silence. 'We have to positively conclude your induction programme, conclude the contracting formalities and then we have to train you to use your new capabilities as soon as possible. You have to review the SS23 specifications. In particular, you will need to study the SS23 interface control document[s] such that you can start to design and build some seeding test equipment. You can start on your own so long by accessing your built-in help files from your built-in main menu. You will find the help files on your internal optical database and you can access the files via your built-in optical Tri-D cube reader. After all of the above we will need to introduce you to the galactic council species working committees so you can work through selected SS23 specifications and sub-system interfaces with them.'

All that Chris could do was to stare at Brian in an idiotic fashion and hope that he would be able to make sense of all this given some time. Then, a thought struck him and he piped up in a querulous tone of voice.

'Why does the galactic council not ensure that there are no unwanted combinations when seeding the planets and in creating seedlings?' Chris asked.

'Even at the atomic level there is choice,' said Brian grimly. 'We are only allowed to ensure that the worst of seedling bugs have been eradicated. In any case the combinations involved are so vast that it is not easy to simulate all of the possibilities. We have to rely on specialist

---

[s] An ICD defines what inputs flow into and out of a process or sub-system.

system testers such as yourself that will tackle the challenge to the best of their abilities.'

After another quad optic piercing glance at Chris, Brian acted after a long pause after realising that Chris could not even think of what to burble.

'Let me show you to your personal cubicle and you can rest and ponder a bit. After all, you did die today,' said Brian with some realisation and measure of compassion. 'The good news is that you have one week of compassionate leave available to you in order to allow you to get used to your new form and to learn how to use your new equipment and your new functions. You will attend an induction programme during that period. Most of your training includes inevitable practising and practising again. Remember that you owe SSTEP a lot of credits for your new form so you can't take forever before you provide SSTEP with some return on investment. You will have to sign a contract with central finance soon if you chose to remain with us. If I were you, I would particularly swot up the full list of prime directives in your help files so you don't end up at the galactic council disciplinary committee inadvertently on a disciplinary charge. Such charges can get you sentience terminated,' warned Brian in a stern voice.

Chris remained flabbergasted, confused and privately panic stricken so he remained silent. He wondered exactly what 'sentience terminated' meant but he felt he could take a nasty guess. Chris trundled off to one corner of the room. Much to his surprise he discovered that he could move! Chris followed Brian on instinct. An aperture in the wall opened in a manner that made Chris think of the iris in a camera and the two master builders moved through the cubicle's door.

One of the two builders exiting the recovery room was in an extremely troubled, disbelieving and confused state of mind. The other seemed to be impatient, bored and surprisingly uncaring. Chris tried hard not to burst into tears, he missed his mom. He wondered if Robots could, or should cry. Did he have tear ducts he wondered?

Chapter Three

(Where Chris Experiments with Some of His Newfound Abilities)

The cubical that they arrived in after some distance of travel in a circular grey corridor was very similar to the recovery room where Chris originally regained consciousness. Grey walls and an iris for a door were in evidence at regular intervals along the corridor. Chris was impressed to see his name glowing on a cubicle's door in green lettering as they drew close. His iris opened into an area that matched the grey ceiling in the same manner as the recovery room where Chris had surfaced. This gave him a strange warm feeling of belonging. It made him think of the days when he was responsible for making a newcomer feel comfortable at work.

'Yes, we try hard to look after our seeding integrators; after all they are our most important asset in more ways than one. It costs a lot of patience, credits, technology and energy to establish a test and evaluation engineer such as you,' observed Brian with a phantom grin.

Chris looked around. A grey rectangle in the middle of the cubicle providing a platform some distance from the floor was obviously a bed. A smaller featureless grey cube next to the bed made him think of a bedside table. A time and date display gleamed in green lettering above the bedside table, some evidence of colour! Chris was surprised to see that the date and time were close to those he had left behind on his Earth as far as he could remember. It seemed to still be late afternoon on the same day of his demise. Faint lines in one wall hinted at a cupboard without door handles and what looked suspiciously like a shower was to be seen in the other corner of the cubicle.

'Why the heck is everything grey?' asked Chris.

'That is the default state,' explained Brian. 'When and if you feel like it you can change the décor to take the form and colour that you like. Do you see the cubicle communication port next to the time and date display?' asked Brian.

Chris trundled closer to the bedside table and saw a circular hairline crack. 'I see it,' he said.

'Unfortunately, you have to interact directly with the cubicle master processor instead of using electromagnetic communication in order to change the décor, that is to enhance your privacy. Try it when you have read up on the procedure in your help files. You can change the forms and colours of everything in your cubicle and you can do things like design and add your own furniture. Just use the communications connection in your left hand. I suggest experiment a bit since the payment credits involved are minimal that compensate for the use of energy,' said Brian earnestly.

'Note that some of your prime capabilities have been disabled in your BP until such time we have been able to complete your induction training. You need to confirm your system capabilities and we need to verify your new and essential eye hand coordination proficiency. We don't want you to accidentally fire your laser in here at full power and mess up a perfectly usable cubicle.'

'Cool,' thought Chris as Brian fiddled with the clock display over the bed.

'I suggest get some rest and let us meet again tomorrow at 08:00, I will meet you here at your cubicle. I have set your alarm for 07:00,' said Brian and moved towards the door which opened silently and then shut behind him before Chris could think to thank him or to wish Brian a good evening.

Chris suppressed an involuntary sudden feeling of panic on being left entirely alone in unfamiliar surroundings. He wondered briefly at the fact that he did not feel hungry or thirsty and was experiencing no need to visit the toilet. Then he remembered what Brian had said about not needing food or the relief from food's consequences. Chris decided that the lack of internal pressure was just as well since there was no toilet in sight and he was missing the normal human appendages he was used to using in the past. He moved over to the bed and sat down on it gingerly. He looked down and noted that the grey material deflected similar to a mattress back home. No blankets or coverings were evident. Chris did not feel uncomfortable since the environment seemed to be at just the right temperature. 'Home?' thought Chris. 'I guess this is home now. I wonder how the heck I access my help files?'

On thinking the thought Chris noticed a display light up in his field of view that made him think of a fighter jet pilot's head-up display. A list of options appeared similar to a computer program's menu structure and Chris could see an item entitled 'Help' and another entitled 'Prime Directives'. He moved his eye's line of sight onto the help option and the option was selected in a manner similar to using a computer mouse. The difference was that there was no need to click. A look and a subconscious command to activate the menu item did the trick.

'Awesome,' concluded Chris. He decided that 'clicking' was not the best term and decided that the word 'designate' best described the menu item selection and activation process, just like a modern fighter pilot would designate a target by looking at the target and by using a head-up display.

A sub-menu was displayed after Chris had designated the help function but Chris could not see the option he wanted namely 'Décor'. As he thought the word and involuntarily imagined the text the option suddenly appeared in his display and it was conveniently pre-designated for him. He read through the illustrated help file text that popped up and realised that there were three simple steps to the process of interacting with the cubicle's main controller. Deploy a communications connection, couple it to the wall connector and then interact with the cubicle's menu system. Following the Tri-D illustrations that described the process, Chris reached over to his left hand, although talon was a better name, with his right hand and pulled on a protective cover on what looked like his index digit. A protective cover opened and Chris pulled out a connector attached to a grey flexible cable. He moved over to the communications port on the wall, touched the circular crack that opened to reveal a circular connector and he made a connection. His head-up display flashed briefly and then was overlaid with a greeting.

'Welcome Mr Chris Petersen and we hope that your stay with us will be a pleasant one. What is your wish?'

Chris suppressed a giggle on the thought that bubbled up in his subconscious of having met a genie in the bottle. He again thought of the word 'décor' and a three-dimensional view of the cubicle appeared, rotating slowly. He designated the wall with the door in it and thought 'colour'. A colour palette appeared and he found that by selecting any colour in the palette just by designating the wall, the wall changed colour instantaneously. Chris concluded that this was a heck of a lot easier and quicker than having to paint walls.

He remembered his childhood days when his brother and he had each been allowed to paint their own rooms. He experimented by firstly choosing the colours that his brother had chosen namely blood red walls and a black ceiling. The result was the same as when he had seen it as a child, garish and depressing. He decided on a white ceiling and four different pastel colours instead, just like his room had been during his childhood. One wall became pastel brown, the next eggshell blue, the next lime green and the last a delicate shade of yellow. He focused his gaze on the floor and thought 'carpets' and he chose a texture similar to that he had left back home. He flushed guiltily on realising that he had not thought about his family up until now. His wife and children had surely heard about his demise by now. He would have to ask Brian how he could check up on them and then he realised that a prime directive disallowed any direct interaction with them. Maybe he could observe how they were doing in a discreet manner? He remembered watching TV and observing a person that claimed he could converse with those that had 'crossed over'. He parked that thought and hoped that his copious insurance policies back on his Earth would help the family now that their breadwinner was toast.

He looked at the grey bed and decided to go for a colour scheme that was similar to the one he was used to at home, a colour scheme consisting of complementary pastel colours that were mostly green and blue. The result was strangely comforting. Chris decided he would add some pictures or paintings and other refinements to the cubicle later and he disengaged the communications link for now. At that instant he became aware of a strong urge to sleep. He resisted the impulse to brush his teeth once he realised, he no longer had any teeth. He felt too tired to even investigate his new form further; his six-taloned 'hands' were going to have to wait for further investigation tomorrow. A cursory examination revealed that he had some form of heating elements in his 'talons' that could be switched on by using his will power as mentioned by Brian. He remembered that the motive behind the design was to stress test specimens after watching some of his talons glowing cherry red for a time. He decided to lie down on the newly decorated bed. On lying down and subconsciously thinking the word 'sleep' the overhead fuzzy white light dimmed and darkness descended. Chris' last thought as he drifted off into familiar and relaxing sleep was related to the overhead light. Could he change the colour to be something else other than fuzzy white? What about a different light shape?

Chapter Four

A musical chime interrupted his sleep followed by soft
feminine voice intoning repeatedly, 'Good morning Chris, it
is time to rise'. Chris mentally shook himself. The voice
ceased and Chris wondered if females in the SSTEP team
were woken with a male voice. He wondered if females also
lost their female parts when they were recruited. He imagined
the female outrage of losing parts to decorate, with
amusement, but then remembered his own response of being
Willie-less and his humour subsided. He swung his legs over
the edge of the bed and spent some time looking at them.
There were the usual number of them but they were grey and
featureless. He wondered if he could customise them in the
same manner that he had used to customise his cubicle. He
decided he would have to consult his help files when he got a
chance. He placed another mental note on his parking lot and
realised he had a built-in calendar and a to-do list. He was not
surprised to see the entries 'Progress with induction training'
and 'Finalise a contract with Central Finance' on the list.

He glanced up at the green clock display that read 07:04 and decided he would change the colour to red at the first opportunity since his alarm clock display at home had been red. Chris realised that he felt a bit homesick. He missed his room and his family, especially his wife and children. The sadness was quite overpowering for a while and then Chris again shook himself mentally. Resisting another impulse to brush his teeth he looked over at the shower cubicle (if that is what it was). Chris moved over to it and one side slid aside on its own.

'I can get used to this automation,' thought Chris. He stepped in but did not see any faucets. The sliding door shut noiselessly behind him. He glanced up and saw that the ceiling and the walls of the cubicle were full of small holes. He was still wondering about that when sprays of water came from all six directions at once and enveloped him. He reacted involuntarily by jumping and tightening his arms close to his body. He swung about somewhat blindly until he realised that the sprays were not a threat. He relaxed his arms and allowed the warm sprays to cover him. He noted that he could detect the water temperature and saw in his head-up display that it was a steady thirty degrees Celsius. It was nice to see that the variables such as temperature were the same as those that he was used to on his Earth. After a few minutes of pummelling the water jets were replaced by warm air. Once the warm air jets shut down the shower sliding door opened and Chris felt like he had just visited a car wash. He realised he was done and he exited the shower. The door slid shut. Chris felt strangely comforted. Having a shower was one of the pleasures he had really enjoyed back home and that was the time he was most creative. This new automated way of doing things was great. There was no need for soaps, shampoos or a wash cloth.

There was no evidence of the typical difficulties associated with the water being too cold or too warm and no water flow sudden changes due to changes in water pressure when someone else in the house used the communal water supply such as flushing the toilet. Chris wondered if he could set the shower parameters such as the pH, the water temperature, the times associated with the spray and the drying-off air period. He concluded that the probability of such optimisation of functional capability being available was very high. He made another note on his electronic parking lot to experiment with the shower parameters when he had some more time. He glanced over at the clock display and realised that it was now 07:24. He concluded that had some time to play with his newfound capabilities after all!

Chris connected himself to the cubicle communications port and experimented with the shower appearance and settings. He decided that thirty-three degrees was more suited to his taste despite not having any skin, along with a longer drying-off period and he set up the parameters accordingly. His help files informed him that cubicle personal preferences had now been set up in a configuration file in his database and could be communicated to any other compatible cubicle that he might visit in future. He noted that his internal database in effect made him a walking encyclopaedia. However, when he attempted to access some of the data in particular relating to teleportation a pop-up message informed him that he did not have the proper authorisation in order to do so and that access was denied.

He changed the shape of the bed from a conventional shape to a circular bed and then made it hexagonal. That looked too ostentatious so he changed it back to the rectangular shape that he was used to on his Earth. He then noted an amount in his head-up display that was negative (and increasingly becoming more negative) and he realised that he was being charged for his changes to his environment. Even here the darn bank was in evidence of ruling his life!

A chime followed by the faintly seductive feminine voice informing him he had a visitor interrupted his experimentation. Brian was requesting permission to enter. 'Let him enter,' designated Chris and the door opened.

'Morning,' intoned Brian. 'How are you feeling? I see you have been able to access your help files,' he approved. 'Looking at your gleaming exterior I see you must have been in the car wash as well.'

'Fine thanks Brian. How are you?' queried Chris with his phantom smile reflecting the fact that Brian had also made use of the car wash analogy.

'Raring to go,' answered Brian. 'Shall we proceed to the training centre?'

Chris remembered he had been told to expect orientation training as was confirmed by his to-do list so he answered in the affirmative. The door iris closed behind them as they moved off down the corridor. Chris was satisfied to see that the door to his cubicle was now a pastel brown and as such a useful landmark to identify his cubicle along the otherwise grey featureless circular corridor with other grey doors. He resolved to think about a different colour and font for his name on the door later on when he was not being crippled by any associated bank charges, slight as they might be.

'You say we can trans-locate to any destination we wish to visit in a rapid matter', said Chris 'so why are we walking?'

'Patience my impetuous friend,' admonished Brian. 'I can do so, but can you? Do you know where to go? Do you have sufficient financial credits? Have you realised that some of your functions have intentionally been disabled?' Chris decided to keep quiet seeing as he was feeling a bit foolish about not having thought the process through far enough.

After about fifteen minutes of moving along the featureless corridor (a corridor interspersed with regular grey doors sporting glowing names that he did not recognise) they passed a door that was an outrageous pink. The pink contrasted with the glowing green name 'Hermien Dunn'. Shortly after that a grey door appeared on the corridor's left entitled 'Training Centre' in orange capitals. Chris noted the use of the orange colour coding and wondered if he should really change the colour of his name on his cubicle since that could mess around with the centre's now obvious colour standardisation policy. The door opened in the now familiar manner of an iris opening and Chris and Brian stepped in. A room that reminded Chris of an IT[t] training room greeted them. The room was full of what looked like computer equipment and the walls were painted with soothing blue, mauve and pink contrasting colours. Chris noted that most of the seats were empty but there were four individuals standing together in a group towards the rear of the training room.

Three individuals all having a 'new' appearance were clustered around a figure that presented an aura of authority,

---

[t] Information Technology

age and wisdom but garbed strikingly different to the rest of the builders.

Brian introduced Chris to the central figure. Chris noted that the figure appeared to be dressed in a suit with a tie but on closer examination the clothing appeared to be painted on or to be part of the figure's exterior. The figure briefly touched Chris' shoulder after being introduced as Olympus their instructor for the day but did not shake hands. Chris concluded that it was best that way since pointing high energy lasers at another sentient individual was not very polite. Thinking of the lack of physical contact also made Chris reminisce about pandemic protection measures on old Earth. Evidently, the transfer of viruses was no longer a consideration to worry about, given the new builder form that did not have any human flesh. The other three individuals looked very similar to what Chris knew he also looked like. Even before Chris was introduced, he somehow sensed that two were female and the other one male although all three exhibited the same nondescript grey exteriors, looking practically identical. Obviously, all builder trainees were of the same build standard and yet were already interconnected in some sort of subtle way yet to be understood.

Mavis, Peter and Hermien were introduced to Chris and Brian and then Olympus asked them all to take a seat. Chris concluded that he now knew exactly where Hermien's cubicle was, now that he could put a face to the pink cubicle after the introductions. Brian excused himself and left after saying that he would fetch Chris later that afternoon. Chris concluded that the other trainees' mentors must have already left after delivering their charges to Olympus, since no other builders were present.

'Welcome to the Persephone Training Centre' boomed Olympus. Chris winced and wondered if all of the master builders were deaf or had a lack of a volume control.

'No, I am not deaf,' responded Olympus. 'I am just making sure you can all hear and I normally do not vocalise a lot these days. I will adjust my volume. Now please pay attention,' he snapped.

Chris made a mental note to find out how he could stop inadvertently broadcasting his thoughts. He shrank a bit into his seat after receiving several amused red glances from the other three trainees.

'It might seem strange to you that we spend time in classroom context when you already have all of what I am going to tell you already in place in each of your databases,' said Olympus in a quieter tone of voice. 'The fact of the matter is that you are all used to this form of instruction and interaction back on old Earth and some BP habits are hard to change even if you have changed your basic form. Old habits die hard. We have found that if we do not initially have this form of interaction with you then the transition to meaningful functioning in your new environment takes longer and involves greater risk to you. We have to do things gradually, since in effect you are children again that will be allowed more capabilities and functions with time. We wish to prevent any accidents along the way.' Olympus paused and looked at each of them sternly in turn.

'Let us not waste words or mince about,' he intoned. 'The greatest danger for any of you is to lapse into depression and be tempted to become sun divers.' The recruits looked at each other in silence but the unspoken question was evident. What was a sun diver?

'A sun diver is a master builder that decides to end it all by intentionally diving into a sun,' explained Olympus. 'I really do not expect anything like that from you given our exhaustive screening including the advanced training and adjusted BP techniques but we cannot exclude the possibility. All of you have lost loved ones and you are now in a totally new but foreign environment. The most important thought I wish to leave you with today is to please speak with your mentor should you ever be tempted to end it all or if you feel overly depressed or find that you are not suitably refreshed after sleeping,' said Olympus sincerely.

'There is nothing that we cannot help you to sort out,' concluded Olympus and he subjected the four trainees to another long piercing look in turn. 'We have only had one sun diver in our collective experience in SSTEP and we believe that by discussing this topic up front we will never have a recurrence,' he stated in a confident tone of voice. The trainees shifted nervously in their chairs and privately hoped that they would never be placed in the situation of being tempted. Privately the discussion was making each one of them a little morbid and sad as memories of old Earth and loved ones came flooding in.

'Now on to more pleasant topics,' intoned Olympus. 'I know that at least two of you have experimented with your help system and you have interacted with your cubicle computers.'

Chris looked at Hermien since the pink door was still vividly in his memory. It was interesting that Olympus knew who had done what and he wondered how. Maybe everyone's negative credits were being monitored? Possibly the cubicles were bugged? Were the recruits under continuous surveillance?

'Use your help functions as much as you can since they were designed to help you through your transition to life at SS23 and to help you to perform your tasks. You will find that as time passes you will need to use your help files less and less. Help files can also be accessed by you without any data charges being incurred. Any questions so far?' boomed Olympus.

'When do we get to learn how to use our communications interfaces properly,' asked Chris still wincing slightly from Olympus' reduced audio volume but still finding it to be a bit loud.

'Well done, that is the next topic,' intoned Olympus after again turning down his audio output slightly in response to Chris' obvious pseudo wince. Olympus explained the communications process and it was really quite simple. The process involved knowing what the address was of the person or group of persons to speak to while mostly avoiding the broadcast address. The broadcast address worked for everyone and was normally only used for emergencies. Chris realised that he had unintentionally been using the broadcast address. Communication was normally initiated when the other party accepted a connection and that was the case except for the broadcast channel. The concepts of telephone conferences and email back home using packets of data on the Internet or data on the global packet radio network came to mind. Chris concluded that the concept was basically simple but he knew that the implementation of such technology was another thing altogether. Regarding communicating properly in practical terms, the greatest problem was in structuring what needed to be said and not broadcasting what one did not want to transmit.

'Exactly' came Olympus' thought to Chris much to Chris' irritation since he believed he was in control and had shielded his private thoughts and was not using the broadcast channel. Chris realised that other subliminal channels must exist. The word 'burble' came to mind and Chris saw his mentor in his mind's eye. A display in his vision came to his attention. Chris realised that he could monitor to whom he was connected to in his communications status field on his head-up display and he also realised he was also currently inadvertently connected to his mentor Brian. He blushed mentally, wondered if he could actually blush, then realised that this matter of proper addressing the recipients of any message was a lot trickier than he thought.

'Well done Chris,' intoned Brian on confirming that Chris had been able to single him out from all of the SS23 personnel on the system integration facility. Chris cut the connection hurriedly and hopefully not too rudely.

'Communicating properly involves thinking through what you want to say and then transmitting it and only it to the correct address or addresses. That is the correct communications etiquette,' concluded Olympus.

Olympus went on to explain each of their newfound capabilities in comparison to their old human build standard on Earth. He started with their new cloaking function. Each of the trainees was shown how they could activate their cloaking field and de-activate it on command. It was strange to see each of the trainees apparently vanishing from sight and then appearing from nowhere at another spot in the training centre. Chris realised that he could still detect that they were there even if his visual sensors could not distinguish them from their surroundings. Olympus intoned that the use of cloaking fields was detectible to master builders from a close range but was mostly undetectable to any other sentient species that were under surveillance and indeed everyone else as well for a range greater than about twenty metres. The trainees were again warned to keep away from satellites and computer systems on planets such as on old Earth due to the potentially destructive electromagnetic interference caused by the cloaking fields.

Olympus explained how the various sensors that each trainee was fitted with operated. Their laser related capabilities enjoyed lively discussion and dire safety warnings were issued regarding its use. Olympus stated that safety first was as important a concept in integration centre SS23 as it was on Earth. The high-energy laser was apparently a new addition to SS23 integration staff basic equipment. Olympus then removed each person's laser-associated BP interlocks and they discovered that they now had a new menu plug-in entitled 'Laser Control'. Each trainee was given a chance to fire his or her laser into a test area that was adjacent to the training centre. It was initially strange to see that targets in the test area were destroyed without any apparent evidence of a laser being fired. Olympus explained that contrary to popular belief on old Earth, practical high-energy lasers did not leave a ruby, green or blue trail when fired. The more powerful lasers operated in the x-ray or infrared bands, activated for short periods of time and emitted radiation invisible to the naked human eye and even master builder sensors. Olympus showed the team how they could however select their sensors to scan the electromagnetic spectrum that they wished to scan, thereby making the laser energy beams more visible. They were no longer restricted to only having daylight capability; their specially designed optics allowed scenes to be viewed in total darkness and even the effects of radio communication energy on the environment could be seen. When the trainees selected their x-ray sensors, beams of radiant energy could be seen when the lasers fired.

Chris was pleased to see that his beam of radiant energy went directly to where he wanted it to go and the designated target vaporised very satisfactorily. On Earth, Chris had been a mediocre marksman with projectile weapons and it was gratifying to see that he now had remarkable eye-hand coordination with no shaking hand. Olympus explained that it was normally not necessary to fire the laser at full power and that it was normally used for fine dissecting or heating work at a fraction of its full power output. Full power was used for amputating items such as damaged mechanical or seedling limbs or aiding in construction work. Chris was intrigued by a question posed by Peter regarding the use of the laser for self-defence and was disappointed when the question was ignored by Olympus. Chris wondered why.

Olympus called a halt and explained that seeing as everyone now had experienced a taste of his or her newfound capabilities it was necessary to contract formally before further progress could be made with the induction process. A chime sounded and a grey entity that looked very much like the trainees entered the Persephone training facility. The trainees were introduced to Portia from central finance. Portia uploaded a thick legal document to each trainee via wiring to each person's communications port and Chris concluded that privacy principles applied in a similar vein to communications with cubicles. Portia had several communications ports and the legal documents were uploaded to each student in parallel, Portia looking like the hub of a wheel in the process.

Each master builder realised that in exchange for their services to SSTEP they were granted basic accommodation, their newfound forms and capabilities with a salary that would render them free from debt in around ten old Earth years. The energy debt having been incurred to grant them their new capabilities. Chris was interested to read about the conditions relating to 'breach of contract' and saw that mention was made of 'enforcers' that had the powers of arrest very much like on old Earth.

Each trainee was requested to affix his or her digital signature to the legalese in the presence of the others as witnesses. No trainee quibbled and Portia left the training centre with the duly notarised digital contracts that Olympus had also countersigned.

'It is time for you to have a short break and then I expect that your Mentors will collect you,' communicated Olympus. Everyone was surprised to note that it was late afternoon. 'We will discuss the prime directives in greater detail tomorrow. Now that you have legal contracts with SSTEP we need to accelerate our training, I am afraid we are a little behind schedule. We will perform a field trip later this week and then we will meet with the galactic council to discuss the SS23 species specifications and the applicable SS23 ICD. Take five while I configure a generic course register template for this course and get you to sign the register electronically. We need to have good training records for the auditors.'

Chris was amused to see the evidence of red tape but was also pleased to see that there was evidence of proper order in the training process in that it could be audited by a third party. The process was far from haphazard and that suited his ordered way of life, it looked like proper order had accompanied him to the SS23 integration centre. Chris thought it to be a lot better this way in comparison to being a child on Earth and to learn things the hard way and despite having two mentors on Earth, a mother and a father. Chris made a note in his parking lot to ask Brian if and when he could meet, or at least speak with, some of his ancestors, once he had found out about who remained alive on his previous family tree.

Chris trundled over to Hermien and asked her how her décor experiments had gone. She smiled ruefully and beamed the thought at him that she had gone a little overboard. They compared credits and Hermien's negative credit was larger than Chris' so he felt a little better about his experimentation and less anxious about his 'kid in a candy store' attitude. Playing with unfamiliar new technology was so much fun! The two trainees experienced a feeling of camaraderie given their shared knowledge and agreed to compare cubicle designs soon. Chris noted that Peter and Mavis were also deep in conversation and he wondered if the situation was accidental or contrived by the instructor or the trainees' mentors. Two pairs of two partners of previous different sexes hitting it off together so quickly seemed a little suspicious, could it be contrived? Chris felt a little concerned about tacit manipulation but decided to not share his paranoia with Hermien. Maybe having opposite sex builders working together was good for moving on to a new life, surroundings and physical forms. Chris reluctantly trundled back to his seat since he wanted to find out more about Hermien, her background and her experiences at SSTEP to date. He hoped that a suitable opportunity would present itself in due time.

Brian and the other trainee mentors arrived and the team broke up into trainee-mentor pairs. Olympus communicated the expectation of seeing them all tomorrow morning at 08:00 in Persephone.

Brian and Chris trundled along the corridor again and Chris wondered about the possibility and scheduling of teleportation training in this week. He also wondered about the items on his parking lot but when he started to ask about them Brian told him to be patient that tomorrow was another day. Chris suppressed a feeling of irritation. He was gratified when there were no comments from Brian as Chris made a rude comment to himself so he knew that he was getting better at communicating! He again directed a question at Brian about the possibility of teleportation since it seemed an innocuous enough question. Brian finally grudgingly responded that Chris would need to have mastered the teleportation function before the field trip that Olympus had previously mentioned. When Chris asked what the field trip was all about Brian answered that it was up to Olympus as to where and when they would be going and he did not want to spoil the surprise. Chris felt petulant but decided to leave it at that and to keep his curiosity in check. It was obvious that Brian was in an introverted, distant and irritated mood this afternoon for some reason. Maybe the SS23 schedule was bothering him.

Brian dropped Chris off at his cubicle with the light brown door with a request that Chris make an early night of it to allow his newly configured digital brain to recuperate from the stress of leaving Earth and his family. Brian left and Chris felt somewhat depressed that he had not received the answers he craved about his family he had left back on Earth. Chris resolved to pester Brian about the topic first thing in the morning, no matter how taciturn Brian might be. Chris also resolved to add some décor to his cubicle's blank walls and wondered if they had DSTV. He giggled at the thought and then thought again. What did people at integration centre SS23 do for fun? His parking lot now had over ten items on it. He decided that he might as well add some pictures to the barren cubicle walls seeing as answers to questions seemed to be unavailable at this time.

Chris trundled over to the communications port above the clock display and started deploying his serial communications cable for connecting to the cubicle computer. Suddenly, he heard a strange crackling sound and his olfactory sensors picked up a smell he thought he could never smell again, the smell of frying electronic equipment. His head-up display filled up with a sequence of red text and an unpleasant foghorn audio alarm pierced his sensitive hearing. The gist of it filtered through to him in that there was an emergency and he was it! Instinctively, he shouted for help on the broadcast channel as his displays wavered, shut down and were followed by blackness.

Chapter Five

(Where Chris Debates the
Seedling Specifications Before
Embarking on a Class Field Trip)

Chris opened his optics to see the familiar grey ceiling with its fuzzy white light. Brian's dome interrupted his vision and Chris beamed a question as to what had happened. There was no response. Panicked, Chris spoke the question aloud and was reassured to hear Brian's grumpy voice.

'Can you believe it?' intoned Brian in a disgusted tone of voice. 'It seems that you like turning yourself into charcoal at every possible opportunity.'

'What happened?' burbled Chris.

'You experienced a major and unplanned system malfunction. One of your Tri-D memory cubes unexpectedly short-circuited and formed a sneak path[u] that directly short-circuited your main power supply. Half of your wiring melted and we were concerned that your reactor might become unstable. Luckily, your fail-safe interlocks activated before you could become a super nova. In effect you have died twice

---

[u] A sneak path is a conductive path that unexpectedly and unintentionally draws current from a power supply.

on two consecutive days since we had to re-configure an entire new processor memory bank for you,' said Brian in a disgusted tone of voice as if it was all Chris' fault.

'No kak!' said Chris. 'How the hell did that happen?'

'Well', said Brian sheepishly 'unfortunately the failure modes and effects analysis on our build standard did not take the possibility of that specific failure into account. No one expected it and we have never seen it before. It was a random failure of the 'component infant mortality' classification. On the positive side, the accident means that we could put in a modification instruction via the build standard configuration management board and it was approved. All the enumerated serial numbers models of our build standard were identified as requiring a modification to Tri-D circuitry to prevent a recurrence of the accident. I guess you have indirectly benefitted all of us since we were mostly built the way you are built. We have all been modified,' stated Brian with a thankful tone in his voice.

Chris pondered that statement and felt strangely content. Being a piece of charcoal had its advantages even if the advantages were indirect.

'Management has waived the cost of your repairs since they were out of your control and therefore the SS23 integration centre will be carrying the cost of your repair,' said Brian quietly.

'You mean I actually get an effing guarantee on my hardware?' asked Chris incredulously.

'You can put it that way I guess,' laughed Brian. 'The good news is that I have performed extensive testing and even an intentional simulated recurrence of the malfunction after the modifications were made and the improvements have held up wonderfully,' said Brian proudly. 'I had to reset your communications protocols and database access codes but I have now restored your state to where you were prior to the accident inclusive of your first hours in SSTEP,' concluded Brian.

Chris initially wondered what recording devices had been used to capture his arrival at SS23 and his experiences after that, then Brian explained that Chris' own memory as activated yesterday had been used. Luckily, that small part of his build had survived the electrical fire resulting from the short circuit.

'Come on let's get to Persephone. We are late for the next part of your training. In case you are wondering note that your intake's training was suspended in accordance with our safety policy to allow your repairs to be completed. As I said, your classmates have already had their new preventive modifications implemented to prevent a recurrence of this rare malfunction thanks to what we have learnt from you.'

The two master builders trundled out of the recovery centre's door and wordlessly trekked down the grey corridor past Hermien's door, a door that was now a more delicate shade of pink. Soon, the orange lettering of the Persephone training centre came into view. They entered to meet the stare of four apprentice builders with their piercing quadruple red optics. Chris could sense many unspoken questions. Chris noted that each of the builders now exhibited variations of integrated clothing and Chris felt a little out of place with his standard grey garb. It was obvious the others had been experimenting with their specialised configuration routines. Chris promoted his to-do list entry relating to experimenting with designer clothing to top of the list. Brian withdrew after greeting Olympus respectfully.

'Ah hah!' exclaimed Olympus. 'Our piece of braaivleis[v] has decided to grace us with his presence.'

Chris grinned sheepishly and shortly recounted what had happened to him to a silent and attentive audience. He particularly enjoyed the solicitous glances being directed towards him by Hermien when he told everyone about the scary feeling of cooking from the inside out and then losing all system power.

'Luckily, I could send an SOS on the broadcast channel and even luckier Brian heard me and could ensure a reactor meltdown in time to supplement the safety interlocks that had been triggered in any case,' concluded Chris thankfully. Each of the classmates then told him that they also heard the distress call and Chris realised just how powerful the emergency channel communication was.

At that point Olympus decided that enough was enough, everyone's curiosity should have been sufficiently satisfied for now. Olympus directed the class to their help files and asked them to view the prime directives. As expected, the directive that was top of the list was the one pertaining to self-determination and Olympus drilled the class mercilessly on its importance, citing the consequences of intervention without due cause and without prior approval. It turned out that the sentence of sentience termination on being found guilty of a prime transgression consisted of having one's database intentionally deleted meaning that the individual

---

[v] Braaivleis translated means barbequed meat in South African terms.

essentially ceased to exist and could not be resurrected in any form.

'Why do we have to have all of this secrecy, surely builders have visited Earth as a part of monitoring human progress?' asked Peter.

'Originally, there was a lot of interaction between humans and builders, however we found that resulted in some builders being classified as gods by the humans. Even worse than that, the technology and training that was provided by builders was abused against their own kind by the humans. Some humans even used some of the technology against builders, resulting in unforgivable harm. The most recent evidence of that was when advanced technology resulted in sparking the second world war on old Earth. Admittedly, that was due to some members of the galactic federation ignoring the quarantine order against Earth as instituted by the ancients,' explained Olympus.

'Who were the ancients and how do they fit in with this galactic federation?' asked Mavis.

'The ancients were responsible for the initial seedings on old Earth. They established several bases on Earth and started expanding various human sub-seedings across the planet. Their first base was situated at Puma Punku[w] and Tiahuanaco in Bolivia, next to Peru. A few other examples of ancient bases are the pyramids in Egypt, Easter Island, Gobekli Tepe

---

[w] Puma Punku is situated high above sea level. Interconnecting stone H-blocks litter an ancient area on old Earth. Some stone blocks are around five metre in size, are precision cut to an extent better than present human technologies and weigh up to 100 tons. The stone quarry is about 100 km from Puma Punku.

in Turkey and the Chichen Itza Mayan Temple in the Mexican Yucatan peninsula. The ancients built the stone seeding coordination centre and team landing site at Puma Punku within 24 hours of their arrival,' intoned Olympus.

'How could the ancients do that?' asked Chris in wonder.

'They arrived on site along with a complete set of engineering designs and assembly steps. They selected a nearby quarry that had sufficiently hardy stone. Andesite[x] stone was selected as the prime building material due to its long-term hardiness. A modular building technique was employed. This technique employed manufacturing groups of interlocking stone blocks called H-blocks that were mass produced in sufficient quantities. The whole structure was assembled on site in a stepwise manner but some parts were completed in parallel,' explained Olympus.

Peter interjected wanting to know how the blocks could have been cut with such precision and how they could have been taken to the Puma Punku site given the distance, the mass of each block and the number of blocks that would have been needed for the huge facility.

'The 3D designs were used to program a small army of Molecular Levitational Cutters. These were used to cut the H-block 3D contours at exact right angles where necessary. Intricate details were carved out and added while the blocks were being held in place by magnetic fields, all while being worked upon. The MLCs then transported the sub-assemblies

---

[x] Andesite is a form of volcanic rock that includes some quartz and has a hardness of 7 on the Moh scale, meaning that it is hard to cut and shape. Diamonds have a Moh rating of 10 and talc a rating of one.

of cut rock to the construction site where they were put in place in accordance with the master assembly plan. Then each MLC returned to the quarry in a cyclic manner to cut and pick up the next block in the sequence for the structure' enthused Olympus.

Chris wondered if modern techniques on old Earth could cut and move stone with the sort of precision and accuracy that the ancients obviously had, tens of thousands of years ago in old Earth's past. He felt that the technology as he remembered it still had a long way to go. He listened attentively as Olympus compared technologies.

'Scientists on old Earth compared the present stone working techniques to those used by the Ancients. A microscopic view of a laser cut leaves an edge on the stone that reveals vitrification[y]. There is no such evidence on any H-block surfaces. A diamond saw leaves minute circular tool mark evidence despite polishing thereafter, there are likewise no such marks to be found on the H-blocks. Polishing takes a lot of time, but there was no time or need for any such finishing step in H-block manufacture. Cutting complex inlays into rock as well as adding precisely spaced holes present a challenge to laser and diamond saw technologies. These older techniques are far surpassed by MLC technology. Lasers and saws take a lot of time to dress stone whereas the MLCs separate planes of rock at the same time in microseconds. In addition, the MLC lifting and transport process does not require any supportive structures such as

---

[y] From the Latin vitreum is the transformation of a substance into a glass. Heating rock for example by a nuclear explosion, turns the surface of exposed rock into a hard glass-like state.

scaffolding or cranes. To add to MLC technology, our builder designs were also crafted by the ancients although there have been several build standard improvements over the years in our case,' explained Olympus.

'Once Puma Punku was complete and functional, many galactic federation council meetings took place there. The nearby Tiahuanaco site was also used for that purpose. Stone head depictions of the various earthly and galactic seeding deliberations that took place at Tiahuanaco deliberations were placed into the stone walls[z] as a tribute and commemoration to galactic cooperation,' Olympus concluded.

'So, what happened to the ancients and why are all of the archaeological sites that we have discussed in a state of disrepair?' Mavis asked.

'It was once again the abuse of technology as provided to the humans.

Almost without fail newer technologies were used to suppress other peoples on Earth and thousands died in wars as a result. The galactic federation decided to impose a quarantine on Earth and its peoples until such time they could work together constructively to everyone's benefit. That meant that all extra-terrestrial structures had to be emptied, abandoned and advanced technologies stripped away. Then vast numbers of builders and seedlings had to be transported from old Earth to elsewhere in the universe. Puma Punku was disassembled by randomly concentrated MLC action. Other

---

[z] The Tiahuanaco Temple has rows of these heads, including a grey head that depicts the involvement of the socalled extra-terrestrial 'Greys' that still visit Earth clandestinely to this day. The meeting site is around 1 km to the northeast of Puma Punku.

seeding sites such as Gobekli Tepe were intentionally buried. That was how the one prime directive came to be instituted. The galactic confederation is waiting patiently to see if the present seedings on Earth will mature and survive, or if they will destroy themselves. The dark teams are trying to facilitate the extinction process and that is why they are a banned organisation.'

Chris asked a further question that diverted the class from the prime directives for a time.

'If I understand correctly, we need to test the designs for the next class of species,' stated Chris and Olympus answered in the affirmative.

'Does that mean that we can make suggestions to improve the design? We have had lots of experience with the current design on old Earth,' said Chris eagerly.

'That depends what you mean,' stated Olympus. 'Often, we find that well-meant improvements have long-term serious and terminal consequences. A short-term gain can have a long-term effect that results in a species not making it,' he warned. 'Maybe you should give us an example of what you mean?' Olympus asked.

'Well, one of the irritating things one has to battle with is to do something while your hands are full. What about having four arms?' asked Chris enthusiastically. He was gratified to see the nods of approval from his classmates.

'That is a perfect case study and it crops up a lot. The answer helps me to illustrate another prime directive, the directive pertaining to not taking the galactic council's designs in vain,' said Olympus.

'Consider the design of people living on your Earth. They have a lot of redundancy built into their design. Consider the advantages of having two identical parts should one eye fail, one ear, one lung or one kidney since there is a backup. A lot of thought went into the design and the design is amazingly fault tolerant and self-healing,' said Olympus quietly.

'Understand however that every design has inevitable trade-offs. Some things cannot be duplicated easily such as having two independent brains due to the inevitable nervous system conflict that results. Two brain hemispheres are sufficient redundancy for the human build standard. You would need to have a brain voting system to resolve conflicts if you had three brains. You have to also consider total seedling system behaviour if a part of the seedling becomes damaged. You have to address how to maintain sentience under conditions of partial sub-system failure such as organ failure. The period of time, the mission period when the seedling is deployed, has to be taken into account. Seedling functions need to be combined where possible to reduce overall build standard mass and reduce the need for energy to move the mass, especially over large distances. As an example, your old human body spends more time peeing than it does having sex so the sex function, although being important and a prime requirement for survival has to play second fiddle to frequently emptying the bladder. Multi-functions have to exist as a reasonable compromise with mass, volume and seedling power consumption. Understood so far?' asked Olympus.

A series of mute nods greeted his gaze. Chris wondered if the council design team had a sense of humour, to run a sewer through an entertainment area, but he kept this thought to himself. Olympus continued.

'In human terms on your home Earth every part that you add to a design requires its own skeletal structure, its muscles, its blood supply and the energy to animate it. The process is exponential in terms of complexity since you need to add nerve connections and cooling. If you are not careful you end up with needing another heart along with a pump synchronisation circuit for the increased blood flow and then another stomach to process food for the additional energy requirement. For every change you have to be careful of the effect on the life cycle of the species, the full period from sperm to worm. Ignoring the stress on the mother of having to deliver an infant that looks like a crab is one thing, but if you look at the complexity of having four arms you will find out that the design is not practical in build standard life cycle terms. For starters think about where you would attach another set of arms to the skeletal structure in a manner that allows items to be picked up efficiently without seriously affecting the rest of the seeding by requiring a bulkier skeleton,' concluded Olympus.

'Surely there must be small changes that one can perform to improve the old Earth's human design then,' stated Chris stubbornly.

'OK name one,' demanded Olympus.

'Well, take the matter of the teenagers having roaring hormones and pimples. Why can't that problem be reduced?'

'You were an engineer and you understand the concept of a 'product life cycle' so I am surprised that you have not yet realised that you must look at old Earth humans from the context of, say, a seventy-year life or mission period expectancy. It is true that we had to build-in an age DNA limiter to limit the life span of that specific seeding to prevent over population, self-extinction, depression or madness but think about the design in practical terms for that mission duration of seventy years. To design for end-of-life conditions and an average skin condition you have to mostly have an initial over-secretion that is balanced by an under-secretion at the end of life. At least the seedling experiences as extensive a middle part of life that is enjoyable and trouble free as far as possible, by using this approach,' explained Olympus.

Chris pondered on that.

Peter jumped in and asked, 'What about preventing obesity, drug and alcohol abuse by adding special BP rules?'

'We learnt that any sentient species that is kept on a planet by gravity has an unconscious and never-ending fight against the gravity and that takes energy. You have to make most things enjoyable to seedlings otherwise nothing happens. Eating becomes mechanical and the species doesn't do it without some form of enjoyment. Without taste buds that also tell the endocrine system when to secrete insulin, to trigger pre-programmed hunger, olfactory sensors to stimulate saliva and appetite, the species doesn't care two hoots about food and then starves to death. So, you have to make it fun to eat and then unfortunately some individuals enjoy it too much and overeat,' said Olympus sadly.

'It remains their own choice and with time most can find a happy balance between need and enjoyment. To comply with the prime directive, we had to hide many Earthly drugs in plants and allow each species to learn how to use them the hard way. We tried to limit drug abuse by making many of the drugs bitter, look garish and have nasty side effects but abuse still occurs. With a freedom of choice directive, you cannot easily commit any species to a specific mandatory course of action, they have to establish their own self-control. You hope that the species eventually learns to find the golden middle road and not to over-indulge. Sex is another case in point,' said Olympus.

'Without sex an organic species cannot procreate successfully over the long term. When we originally told a new seeding prototype that we expected males to stick their penises into the female's vagina to transfer sperm there was a horrified response at a process considered barbaric. We could think of no better process despite having several brainstorming design review sessions. So, we had to make the process enjoyable and make it one of the prime driving factors built into the species' BP. This means that the process had to be considered normal and so would result in compliance with the real requirement for the sexual act namely procreation,' Olympus concluded.

'What about the other prime directives', asked Hermien timidly, 'are we going to discuss those as well?'

'Yes,' answered Olympus. 'Let's consider one more for now. The galactic council is mostly powerless to stop the actions of the dark teams as regards the intentional and sometimes spiteful attacks on the SS designs. On the one hand functionality is specified and implemented in the design as specified but on the other hand design attacks take place that are aimed at destroying, copying or damaging the design. Some of our actions in response maintain order and balance between the two opposing forces. In order to damage any new design, the dark teams need to have intimate knowledge of our new designs and they often try to steal in order to get them. The galactic council does not take it lightly if any SS team member passes on any species design information, specification or ICD details either wittingly or unwittingly since the consequences can wipe out a whole new seeding and ruin thousands or millions of hours of work. That is why you have a non-disclosure agreement in the contract that you signed when you arrived here at SS23. In fact, there is an automatic disciplinary hearing to investigate the possibility of any design leak even if there is only a chance encounter with any member of the dark team,' said Olympus seriously. 'You are warned to report any such encounter immediately should one occur.'

'Say!' exclaimed Chris. 'That sounds just like the Missile Technology Control Regime back on old Earth! There are serious penalties if a company passes on classified missile design information to other countries. The other countries are of course quite prepared to pay a lot of money for the information if you do.'

'Exactly,' confirmed Olympus and then changed the topic.

'We need to discuss and confirm the SS23 seeding strategy. We have been lucky to find the planet that we are on and it is very similar to your Earth. Planet 23 also has an oxygen-based atmosphere with similar gravity. Day, night and seasonal changes in the environment are likewise very similar. That is another reason why you have been recruited to form part of the STEP team dedicated to the SS23 initiative. The new seeding that we are working on, is essentially an improved version of the form that you had on old Earth.'

There was an immediate jumble of burbles that greeted this statement, with team members complaining that seeding designs were meant to be fixed and not allowed to be tampered with. Olympus explained that the council was mandated to improve existing designs in a controlled manner and all changes for an improved seeding would be based upon previous build shortcomings and lessons learnt, such as avoiding the effects of cancer. Another change to the previous Earth's design that was being considered for SS23 was a change to the brain structure to make it a parallel processor instead of a serial processor. An improved arithmetic logic unit function was being considered. These additions were likely to increase brain volume and the consequences of that were being evaluated. The impact on this seeding was still under analysis by the strategic seeding analysis team, taking issues into account such as the additionally required brain blood flow and the need for appropriate seeding cooling strategies. A variant of the upgrades being considered was to allow the use of some of digital capabilities, to possibly enable flight in oxygen and other atmospheres. Olympus continued his lecture after the amazed burbling had abated.

'We need to discuss the specialised equipment that you have been provided with in order for you to be able to test SS23. Let's start off with the ultrasound and heating capabilities built into your appendages. How many of you have heard of the concept of environmental stress screening?'

There was a period of silence before Chris indicated that he knew what was meant. He explained that if any system or sub-system assembly was vibrated and subjected to temperature cycles, that is a low temperature alternated with a high temperature, then inherent design or workmanship flaws could be identified early and could then receive proper attention. ESS facilitates reliability growth, meaning that designs could be improved if failures could be detected and rectified early.

'That is a good summary,' said Olympus. You have been provided with ESS capabilities instead of having to rely on external ovens and mechanical so-called shakers like you would need to do on your Earth. You have some built-in ESS testing capabilities!' concluded Olympus triumphantly. He glanced around at the class and noted their stunned silence. He decided to drop the next bombshell related to new functions that the trainees had been given.

'It is time for you to master a new skill namely the skill of teleportation,' he said as he once again performed the magic of enabling a part of each student's BP. A new menu became available in all of the trainee head-up displays entitled 'Transit' and all of them accessed this new menu with curiosity.

'You will need to perform field visits to test subjects at considerable distances from our SS23 integration facility, even off-planet. You might need to visit your old Earth to consider evaluating an improved seeding there as well as here. You will see that you can now access a map of the solar system around this planet by communicating with the SS23 central universe database and downloading the three-dimensional areas of interest. Access to the central maps is controlled according to rights that are granted to specific individuals. Access to specific electronic maps is granted to you depending on your tasks and the need to know. If you look at the map scale and your own position as marked on the map, you should realise that you are currently about ten light years away from old Earth'.

More stunned silence greeted this revelation.

'Why?' squeaked Mavis.

'We need to obey the self-determination directive so we have to keep a respectable distance from Earth and their sensor systems such as their satellites, the Hubble Space Telescope, radio telescopes and radar. You will notice that we are on the far side of a non-revolving planet relative to the sightline from Earth. This centre's planet behaves similar to Earth's Moon in that the planet does not rotate about its axis and the planet is pretty much static in its position relative to Earth. This helps us to cloak our activities from Earth since we have this planet's mass between us and Earth's sensor arrays, their satellites, ground telescopes and the Hubble and James Webb Telescopes. Similarly, our other sentient species seedings are grouped at several locations around the galaxy and spaced far enough apart not to interfere with each other.' Sensing an unvoiced question Olympus answered it before it was asked.

'Yes, there are many sentient species in this galaxy, many have evolved in parallel with the human and other build standards, why should the colony on old Earth be an exception given so many billions of billions of planets in the universe?' he asked sharply.

Olympus was greeted with silence so he grunted approvingly and moved on. 'It is true that planets that resemble you Earth are hard to find and the probability of their existence is tiny. However, with so many galaxies in the solar system, even a tiny probability still yields many potential new seeding sites. It is unlikely for anyone to win the Lotto on old Earth due to the one in fourteen million chances, but somebody mostly does. OK, enough of this for now, let's move on. As I said, you will need to perform field trips across vast distances. You will do this after you have performed tests here at SS23 on sub-systems of the new SS23 seeding such as the heart sub-system, the liver sub-system and the brain sub-system. You will need to design and implement specialised test equipment and test setups to test each part of the SS23 seeding. More details will be provided soon. First let's address the aspect of teleportation.'

'You are now going to learn how to plot a course to a point in space defined by galactic coordinates and then we are going to translocate to a specific coordinate set point as a team. Open your waypoint navigation sub-menu on your transit menu. For now, we are only going to use two galactic waypoints, where we are now as our return waypoint and where we are going to as our destination waypoint. Always remember to define a return waypoint since your BP is programmed to return you to it automatically in case of danger or any of your sub-systems malfunctioning during the away trip and assuming that you would be unable do so on your own. Our destination is old Earth's Moon, the site where Neil Armstrong and his team landed in 1969.' Astonished glances greeted this statement.

'You are lucky in that I was permitted to choose this site since it is so close to your Earth. There is an unusually high level of sunspot activity at this time so we know that our arrival will remain undetected against the anticipated backdrop of electromagnetic noise. We will remain there for five minutes and then our return waypoint will activate automatically and we will rendezvous back here.'

Olympus showed the trainees how to select the required waypoint attributes associated with the location in mind. The attributes included the height above the moon's surface and that was set at five hundred metres above the landing site of the lunar lander. The trainees dutifully designated the destination galactic coordinates on their electronic maps and the coordinates were transferred to their navigation menus. The default attribute of <cloaking on> was retained and the <hover> attribute was also selected. Olympus explained that their guidance computers would hold the group geostationary above the moon and that the group would be cloaked on arrival as a result of this programming. The <time at waypoint> attribute was set to five minutes and the <next step> attribute was set to <return home>.

'Right' said Olympus with satisfaction. 'Now we just need to file our flight plan with the traffic controller at central and we can activate the program once we receive permission to continue'.

Olympus showed each team member how to request the flight plan log with central control by designating the <Approval Request> menu option and each trainee uploaded the flight plan to the traffic controller. A green acknowledgement flashed across each trainee's head-up display to indicate that the trip was confirmed and authorised.

'OK,' said Olympus. 'When I count to three designate your <Engage> function. Please do not speak with one another while we are on site in accordance with our non-interference prime directive. One, two, three.'

On the word 'three' each trainee designated as instructed and experienced a sudden jarring followed by a short period of blackness. Personal displays blinked out to black for a short time and when their displays re-appeared, they found they were looking down on a breath-taking view. Earth shone in all her glory on the horizon and the lunar surface below was bathed in white solar radiation. Chris found that he could rotate slowly on subconscious command and realised that he could also zoom his optical sensors to focus on the criss-crossing set of footprints far below, several obliterated by the primitive chemical rocket exhausts. A display indicated that the radiation levels were high, no doubt due to the abnormally high level of the sunspot activity that Olympus had mentioned. He zoomed in his field of view to realise he was luckily looking at a single perfectly undisturbed footprint despite previous rocket exhausts as probably made by Neil, his team-mate or other Lunar visitors many years ago. Looking at the origin of the footprint trail Chris could clearly see the partially blackened lunar lander module, the part that had been jettisoned when the astronauts blasted off on their return journey to Earth. A second jarring and a brief period of a black display interrupted Chris' reverie regarding the fantastic technical achievement of that time. Chris looked around to see that they were back in the Persephone training room. He turned to see that the other trainees were looking at each other with dazed expressions. Olympus looked on with a smug air.

'Welcome back,' he said. 'You have just completed a twenty-light-year field trip with success. Congratulations.'

There was an instant babble of voices as each trainee burbled away in response to the awesome experience. No one was listening to anyone else but it was obvious that Olympus was enjoying every minute of the trainees' responses to the trip. Each trainee also received a private message of congratulation from his or her mentor and the team's positive spirit could almost be cut with a knife.

After a time, Olympus called for quiet and then made an announcement. The mentors would not be fetching the trainees; they were now capable of translocating to their cubicles on their own. Each trainee found that by zooming in on his or her electronic map of the SS23 integration facility, that they had access to a map of the complex. Each person's cubicle was clearly marked on the map.

It was close to midday but nevertheless the trainees were given the afternoon off and were encouraged to get to know each other better in the special free time that had been granted. With a statement hoping that everyone would enjoy the rest of the afternoon Olympus vanished and everyone was aware that the master trainer had retired to a location of his choosing for some privacy. The four students looked at each other owlishly and then Hermien made the suggestion that they all visit her cubicle seeing as it was the closest. Chris realised that old habits die hard, in that any location within a million kilometres of where they now were 'close' but kept the thought to himself. It appeared that only translocations away from the SS23 planet required traffic control authorisation. The four trainees agreed to rendezvous outside Hermien's door and were there instantly. Chris wondered how they avoided arriving at the exact same spot, since that could result in a mess of trainee part fruit salad, but decided that some aspects of this new technology were incomprehensible to him and best left alone for now. Obviously, safety interlocks were engaged automatically to prevent any fruit salad happening.

Hermien opened the door and they all trooped in. No one remarked on the fact that there was an understanding that cubicles were private but that one could translocate along corridors at will. It was obvious that this was understood by all and considered to be self-evident.

It was also obvious that Hermien had been experimenting at length with her cubicle configuration. She was visibly nervous as regards the reaction from her classmates, a little shy that they would think her ostentatious or being a know-it-all. Everyone took pains not to be too critical and realised that they could sense her emotions due to her being close by. The soft feminine touch was to be seen everywhere from the intricate lace curtains across the non-existent but simulated windows, the mountain view, the ornaments and the highly detailed paintings on the walls. Chris noted that Hermien had opted for conservative wall colours. Soft pink pastel wall shades accompanied a white ceiling. A piece of furniture stood in one corner of the cubicle and Chris realised that it had to be an upright piano. The highly polished top surface was offset with a doily and a vase filled with red carnations.

Small ornaments on the bedside table offset an object and Chris decided that could only be a framed photograph or something very similar. Chris wandered over to a painting on the wall and was impressed with the high level of detail. Brush strokes were in evidence in a view of a laughing woman holding onto a large straw hat while running through a green field interspersed with white dainty flowers. The flowers contrasted with the bright green grass and the dark brown striped mountainous rock formations in the distance with the whole being set against a mauve sky. Chris wondered how Hermien had been able to achieve such a level of artistry so soon. When he asked her, she explained that there were several default paintings and furniture templates that could be selected via the cubicle controller décor palettes. Chris made a note to explore the library when next he was playing with his cubicle's design. Chris moved over to the bedside table where Mavis was looking at a picture of a man and a woman standing next to two children.

'This is fantastic,' gushed Mavis. 'This must be you and your husband with your family. How did you manage to get a picture now that we are here?' she burbled.

Silence greeted Mavis and everyone stared at Hermien until they realised that she was far from an articulate frame of mind. Waves of sorrow were washing over her and despite the silence the other three trainees could feel how deep Hermien's sorrow was at having lost her loved ones. That triggered feelings of sorrow in themselves and a desire to console one another. Chris moved over to Hermien and attempted to give her a supportive hug. It was then that he realised his and her new forms were not particularly conducive to this form of activity. The loud clang as body parts met each other in strange entangled combinations was so comical that both of them burst out laughing.

'Sorry,' said Chris.

'That's OK', said Hermien, 'it was kind of you to want to help and at least I feel a bit better.'

It was obvious that the trainees had a lot to get used to as regards the way of life in integration centre SS23. Chris realised that in a sense they had been re-born and a new set of rules and etiquette applied to everyday life.

Hermien answered Mavis' question about the photograph of her family by explaining that she had found a useful menu tucked away in their new operating system. The 'Screenshot' menu allowed images in memory and to be transferred in digital form to the cubicle computer for purposes of applying décor to one's cubicle. The cubical controller also provided a picture frame as a part of the customisation process. The trainee quartet were awed by the technology involved and there was another period of silence while they digested the implications of this newfound capability where digital constructs could be made to take on a physical form. The process they understood, was termed tridy printing.

Chris made an analogy of having a picture as a background on a computer desktop versus being able to apply the same technique to one's surroundings. He realised that if he wanted to, he could apply a still image to the walls of his cubicle. He also realised that the need for keeping good records of technical tests on SS23 must be the reason why this photographic and tridy printing functionality had been built into them. They could photograph their surroundings at will and save the resulting image, use the result at will, replicate and retain the data for subsequent use and audit.

Chris mused that there was no need to stick with the four colours he had chosen for the walls to his cubicle; he could have a mountain scene for example on one wall and any other scene he wanted elsewhere. He wondered if the scenes could be dynamic, could one have a moving picture decorating the walls and ceiling in real time like a movie? He again parked this thought to experiment further when he was back in his cubicle. Chris then remembered painfully that his personal appearance was still a bland grey when he peeked at his to-do list whereas all of the other trainees had changed their appearance to reflect styles similar to those they had left behind on old Earth. The introverted Peter was wearing what appeared to be a black suit with a tie and Mavis sported a smart steel-blue jacket with a skirt. Hermien was gaily dressed in a white and red polka dot ensemble that made her look very festive. Chris noted that Hermien was looking pensive again and decided to ask her what was troubling her.

'I am worrying about my family,' she explained. 'The car crash that killed me seriously injured my husband but he will survive from what my mentor tells me. Luckily, the kids escaped with minor scrapes and bruises except for my son's broken collarbone. They will all be ok soon; I just wish I could be there and to tell them not to grieve since I am fine,' concluded Hermien sorrowfully.

Chris told the team about his own experiences with the live terminal back on Earth and also expressed his concern about not being able to speak with the family he had left behind.

Mavis spoke up tentatively and said that she had spoken with her mentor on the topic of providing support to those left behind. Her mentor had confirmed that direct contact with one's previous family was forbidden. The need to maintain the myths surrounding death while supporting the prime directives and the need for law and order on old Earth prohibited such contact. There were some people on Earth however that had been given limited communications abilities as gifts or as a part of natural evolution. Actually, all people on Earth had some form of advanced communications abilities that were sometimes seen to have a psychic nature, but the abilities had been intentionally suppressed until the seeding had achieved the required level of maturity. The existing abilities for people on Earth were thus mostly restricted by design.

There were the inevitable charlatans on Earth that pretended to have the communications abilities 'with the other side' in order to be able to dupe trusting victims on

Earth. For that reason, people on Earth had to choose whom to believe and if the right medium were chosen at the correct place and time then loved ones back home could communicate with those that had 'crossed over' in a limited manner. In practise however few families tried to communicate over the divide and such interactions were somewhat discouraged at integration centre SS23 and elsewhere. Chris archived his wish of trying to interact with his family on Earth via a 'medium' for later. He still felt he wanted to discuss the various possibilities and what would be allowed with Brian when he had an opportunity.

Chris noted that Peter had been extremely quiet and uncommunicative all of the time that the team had been together so Chris decided to direct a question at him.

'Say Peter,' asked Chris, 'what job did you do on Earth?'

Peter hesitantly explained that he worked in a protected workshop when he died and he did not have any family, having been abandoned on the steps of a church shortly after birth. He had been a project manager before that at a defence contractor business but was involved in a car accident that left him with severe head injuries. Those injuries eventually caught up with him and his severe migraine attacks turned into a fatal stroke. Chris realised that Peter had become a State Pensioner and that could only mean that he had become mentally challenged as well as being initially abandoned. Peter subsequently volunteered this information and then said with a radiant smile that he could now again do arithmetic and understand how mechanical items such as a laser worked! Back home on Earth he could barely write his own name and he had to rely on shop till operators to not cheat him. Once Peter started talking the wonder and gratitude for this new life at the centre shone through. Chris felt guilty about not having thought about it that way before and not being more appreciative for the fact that he could still function similarly to what he had done on Earth, in fact function a heck of a lot better! On that note the team decided to split up and vanished to their cubicles directly with Hermien's consent and farewell, leaving her to her solitude, privacy and a time to rest.

Chapter Six

(Where Chris Tries to Visit
the Cassini Crash Site)

After Chris arrived in his cubicle he sat on his bed and reflected upon the day's experiences. He concluded that they were incredible and unbelievable. The proof was around him however and he copied Hermien in that he had the cubicle controller provide him with a framed photograph of himself with his family. Playing with the tridy printer was fun! He reverently placed the portrait next to the bed on the featureless bedside table and sorrowed awhile. He reflected once again on the possibility and advisability of contacting his family via a medium on Earth and the thought 'life must go on' came to mind. He had provided for his family adequately and in addition there was the company insurance scheme that would ensure that they would have a comfortable existence. There was now proof that they could meet again someday in some way (even clandestinely) and Chris took consolation in the thought. The pain of separation was temporary. A thought struck him to ask Brian if his family was being digitally monitored and if so, would any of them have a place in the SS23 facility? Given the specialist nature of SS23 he had his misgivings on that score, he wondered about the selection process and how needed capabilities were identified and the recording process funded.

He finalised his cubicle experiments by placing a picture of his Earth's Moon as seen today on the entire wall behind the bed and he found that he could animate parts of that scene. He added small fishes and giggled at the simulated background as the fish swam within the confines of the wall boundaries amongst the moon's valleys and craters. This was fun!

He reflected on the team's recent trip to Earth's Moon and he was awed once again. He concluded that the master builders took great pleasure in viewing the advances made by humans on old Earth that then surely applied to all species and seedings, otherwise why would Olympus have selected the lunar lander site for the field trip? That made Chris think about Star Trek stories back home (he was an avid Science Fiction fan) and other real space probes launched from Earth. Probing space had immense potential and he felt very curious. One particular probe came to mind; a man-made robot probe sent to Saturn called Cassini. The Cassini probe was unique at that time in that it carried a nuclear reactor as its power source and it used celestial 'slingshot' manoeuvres (using interplanetary forces caused by planet masses dragging on the probe's mass to increase its speed), speeding up the probe sufficiently to reach Saturn in the fastest way (and even then, it took years). The SS23 teleportation technology was sure far ahead of that used on old Earth!

The probe had sent many images as well as sensor data back to Earth. He remembered seeing pictures of Saturn's rings on the internet as well as acoustic graphs showing the micro meteorite impacts on the space probe as it flew through

Saturn's rings. Then a thought struck him. He now had the capability to visit Saturn and honour the advances made by humans regarding the probe to Saturn just like the SS23 team had recently done regarding the moon probe! Cassini had been intentionally crashed into Saturn by its mission controller once the probe had reached the end of its useful life. It would be fun to see what remained of the wreckage and if any resulting contamination had taken place at the crash site.

He accessed his galactic map and found that Saturn and its moons were easy to locate. He experimentally set a course to within a few million kilometres of Saturn in a similar manner the team had done earlier that day when visiting Earth's Moon. He set his cubicle as the return address and designated the <Approval Request> button. As soon as he had done so he realised that he had inadvertently transmitted a flight plan request to the traffic controller! He was still wondering how to retract his flight plan to Saturn when a green 'Approved' message flashed across his display. He could not believe it and he agonised over what to do next.

'What should I do' he thought and then realised here was the opportunity he had dreamt about while on Earth, he could travel where he wanted to at will! Bravely, he designated the <Engage> button to experience the now familiar jarring feeling and the short period of blackness while his displays disappeared. When his displays reappeared, he was greeted with the blackness of space interspersed by sparsely positioned brightly lit spheres of light. The nearby planet with the rings about its middle could only be Saturn and Chris was stunned at the magnificence of the view. He looked down and experienced a sudden feeling of panic and vertigo when he realised, that he was on his own in the middle of space with nothing to stand on. He found that he could revolve almost unconsciously as and when he wanted to and the vertigo left him since he realised that he was fully in control. He remembered his original goal of wanting to view the Cassini probe and he realised guiltily that he had not thought of finding out where the probe had crashed so he could avoid any Earth sensors or other probes that might be active in the area, in accordance with his prime directives. What would the people back home do if they experienced a probe malfunction due to his cloaking field! He was thankful that he had remembered to switch on the <cloaking> attribute in his flight plan.

He started hoping fervently that his cloaked structure was not interfering with any remote sensors or any local sensors that might be around as regards their onboard equipment. He spent some time scanning space around himself and looking at the surface of the planet with his optical sensors, hoping to see evidence of the Cassini probes demise. After a few minutes of looking around himself, like a pilot moving his head around in a jet fighter cockpit, he realised that this process was fruitless. This was worse than looking for a needle in a haystack since this haystack was incredibly huge.

He decided to use his electromagnetic sensors in a scan around himself since he knew that any other probe or satellite in the area must be transmitting to old Earth. After a time, he located a moving object with a radio signature that could only be another probe. Thankfully, it was a considerable distance away and Chris zoomed into the object with his optics to reveal the outlines of the probe with its array of solar panels and antennas. Chris was immensely gratified as he calculated the probe's flight path to realise that the probe was thankfully moving away from his current position where he was hanging in space. He zoomed his optical sensors away from the probe with the intention of getting a closer look at Saturn and then he realised that there were three other objects in space moving close to his location!

The three objects were cloaked and from that he could conclude that they were similar in construction to him. They were behaving strangely in that they were moving directly towards him and he had the feeling that they were towing a device between them that seemed to be threatening in nature, could it be some form of grappling device? Chris was at a loss in that he did not want to initiate any communication. He had a concern that it might interfere with the Earth probe that he had detected or that he would be detected and that he would break a prime directive. The advance of the three objects was however obviously threatening in nature and Chris' instincts took over. He opened up his laser menu and fired a warning shot at the grappling device that the three entities were dragging between them and was astonished at the result. The device and all three of the objects lit up with a sudden incandescence that overloaded his optics and left him blinking owlishly at space that was now devoid of movement. All three objects along with their grappling device had vanished!

Chris spent several minutes trying to understand what had happened and then he decided to trigger his return waypoint. Soon he found himself back in familiar surroundings. His empty cubicle greeted his gaze and he sank down onto his bed thinking furiously.

Chapter Seven

(Where Chris Has to 'Please Explain')

Chris realised after a time that there was a possibility that he had met with hostile entities similar to his build standard, maybe members of the dark team? He remembered his mentor's instructions that all contacts with the dark Teams had to be reported and would be investigated. Exactly what the investigation involved Chris had no idea but he decided that he had best comply with his instructions. He thought about the most effective manner of telling Brian what he had experienced and then he directed his thoughts at Brian by using his new communications abilities. He addressed Brian and was relieved to hear the now familiar acerbic tones of Brian's voice.

Chris started off hesitantly by telling Brian that he had undertaken a trip to Saturn and Chris was amazed at the immediate reaction.

'What!' roared Brian in shocked tones. 'Stay where you are, I will be there in a moment.'

Chris was surprised at Brian's lack of decorum when he appeared inside Chris' cubicle. Brain had not bothered to use the normal route via the corridor with its door. Brian fixed Chris with his piercing quad optic red glance and instructed him to relate what this was about having completed a trip. Chris hesitantly told how he had been experimenting with his programmed flight menu and how surprised he was when his flight plan was authorised when he accidentally designated the <Approval Request> menu button. Brian interspersed Chris' narrative at this point with another disbelieving roar before telling him to continue.

Chris told Brian about the initial difficulties due to his lack of planning that he had experienced in finding the Cassini probe crash site and how thankful he was when he located another probe some distance away and to realise it was moving away from him. Brian snorted and Chris wondered what that meant. Chris moved on to the encounter with what he took to be dark teams and watched as Brian's quad red irises expanded momentarily when he spoke about the sudden burst of energy that resulted from the firing of his laser. After Chris finished his story describing how Brian had been contacted almost immediately after the trip. Brian sat silently for several minutes before making an earth-shattering statement.

'I am afraid that I have to place you under immediate suspension pending a disciplinary hearing,' he said quietly. 'You are confined to your quarters and I am afraid I have to block all of your advanced capabilities until further notice. You will be fetched when you need to appear before the central committee.' Brian vanished before Chris could say anything.

Chris sat on the bed in an almost paralysed state of mind. He thought back on the recent events and felt that he had not really done anything wrong. He checked his menu system to discover that several menus were indeed missing as Brian had indicated. Chris started feeling sorry for himself and a little apprehensive as to what would happen next. His reverie was interrupted by his familiar cubicle female voice indicating that there were visitors at the door, so and he instructed the door to open.

Two black imposing figures entered that he had never seen before and one of the two requested that he accompany them. These could only be enforcers. Wordlessly, he rose and left his cubicle with trepidation, the door iris closed behind the trio silently. They moved off down the corridor in the opposite direction to the training centre with a black figure on either side of Chris. He experienced a spark of interest since they were moving in an area he had not visited before but then a feeling of gloom descended upon him and he once again started feeling sorry for himself. The trip was over suddenly when the trio arrived at a door having a light mahogany wooden look to it that was labelled 'Boardroom'. The trio stood outside the door and waited a time before the leader of the two guards turned to Chris and told him to enter. The enforcers stationed themselves outside and on either side of the door as Chris stepped in hesitantly.

He was greeted with the sight of twelve seated entities in a semi-circle grouped around a single chair. He was asked to sit down by the central figure in the semi-circle. Chris looked at the group and thought he could identify Olympus as being the last entity on the left. Chris had no idea as to the identity of the rest of the entities and he looked at each with trepidation. The central figure that had asked him to sit spoke again.

'I am the Jason, the SS23 facility CEO and this is the SS23 central management committee that you see before you. I regret having to meet with you in this manner seeing as I have not the chance to meet with you previously as a new recruit,' intoned the solemn chairperson.

Chris was at a loss as to what to say so he remained silent. Jason paused for some time and kept his gaze fixed on Chris for some time, causing Chris' discomfort level to increase.

'You have the right to representation at this hearing and I would like to suggest that you consider accepting your mentor Brian in this role. Do you agree?'

Chris then saw that Brian was standing to the right of the semicircle when Brian stepped out of the shadows cast by the subdued lighting. Brian looked at Chris and nodded slightly.

Chris firmly answered, 'I concur.' Brain moved over to stand behind Chris.

'In that case let us begin,' said Jason and he again stared at Chris for a period of time that seemed like an age to Chris. 'You are charged with embarking on an unauthorised teleportation trip, embarking on an improperly planned trip that could have resulted in the disclosure of our presence to the humans on Earth via one of their probes and the passing on of technical detail pertaining to your build standard to the dark teams. How do you plead?'

Chris indignantly replied, 'Not guilty.'

Jason nodded and turned his gaze upon Brian. 'What defence do you offer?' he asked.

'We contend that the trip was not intentional, that authorisation was indeed given and that the resulting contact with the dark teams was actually planned by the dark teams,' intoned Brian.

This statement astonished Chris and he turned around slightly to look up at Brian.

'I request that Chris be allowed to provide the council with his account as to what happened in order that the claim we make can be substantiated,' Brain requested.

Jason was silent for a time and it was clear that he was communicating with the rest of the council in a manner that excluded Chris and Brian. After a time, he turned to Chris and instructed, 'Continue.'

Chris addressed the council hesitantly explaining how he followed the same process that had been followed when the trainees had teleported to Earth's Moon. He explained that he was rehearsing the process and had not intended to request the traffic controller to authorise the trip. He mentioned that he was greatly surprised when the inadvertent trip request was authorised. The temptation to proceed was too great and he initiated the trip accordingly. He only realised that he had not adequately considered the location of the Cassini probe once he arrived close to Saturn. He had checked for the presence of all probes in the area and he was relieved to see that the only probe in the area was sufficiently far away and was moving further away from him. The presence of the three dark shapes with their grappling device startled him; he did not want to compromise his presence by attempting to communicate with them. He activated his laser in self-defence and was totally unprepared for the result when there was a blinding detonation.

Silence greeted Chris,' testimony and he could see that the council was silently abuzz. Jason turned to Brian and asked him if he had anything to add and Brian spoke up.

'Chris is a new recruit and as such still has a lot to learn. The traffic controller should not have authorised the trip. The traffic controller knew about the Cassini probe, old Earth spacecraft and the possibility of disclosure in violation of the prime directives. The contact with the dark team was not premeditated by Chris and he reported the contact immediately after his return. That should count in mitigation,' explained Brian.

The council deliberated. Jason asked Chris why he had fired his laser at the grappling device and Chris responded by stating that the advance by the three dark shapes gave him the impression of being threatening. He had wanted to protect himself by firing a warning shot. He had not expected the resulting flash that overloaded his sensors and that signalled the end of the three dark shapes along with their strange device. Jason indicated that the council wished to investigate further testimony and he adjourned the hearing, asking Chris and Brian to remain where they were. The council members vanished and Chris and Brian looked at each other owlishly in the empty boardroom.

'Thanks,' said Chris.

'Thank me later,' said Brain. 'It isn't over yet.'

A chime sounded after a prolonged wait and the council members reappeared.

'This hearing is once again in session,' Jason stated.

'It has been established that our presence was not compromised on old Earth after we investigated the human telemetry links and the data recorded by the probe that you found. Thankfully, the probe's sensors were directed away from the flash that signalled the destruction of the three dark team members. The traffic controller has subsequently confessed to illegal contact with a dark team and has been immediately sentience terminated as a result. It appears a grudge was borne against the council for a previous misdemeanour on the controller's part resulting in previous disciplinary action. Revenge was sought. Details of your Cassini mission flight plan were intentionally leaked to the dark teams and they hoped to capture a specimen of you, our latest build standard, for analysis and possible copying. Your advanced laser capability came as a surprise to them and you were lucky to hit their grappling device power supply dead-on. They are unlikely to have had any opportunity to report what happened to their superiors so our design detail is unlikely to have been compromised. Congratulations.'

'Thank you,' said Chris faintly.

'As regards disclosing your presence to humans in future, you have to be more circumspect at this time. They can detect you more easily these days than you think. Radar and visual sensors on old Earth are becoming more sophisticated; the humans are coming of age and might be allowed to join the galactic federation once they have properly matured. There are three instances of mishaps in this regard that have happened recently. The humans have actually detected two of our craft and placed video recordings on their news networks. The United States Air Force released a declassified video showing one of our craft performing manoeuvres that would smash any human form. In that case the builder forgot to cloak his craft. The second video was taken by a Chilean helicopter pilot of a mothership while it was in its cloaked state. The Chilean Airforce was testing a new infrared video camera and the craft was detected by pure chance[aa].'

[aa] A large craft was detected at a range of 35 km from the Chilean helicopter that could not be seen using the helicopter's normal daylight video camera. When the pilot switched to his infrared

'Another thing to remember is that you could be detected purely by performing actions that are beyond human capabilities. Their state of advancement or technology readiness is advancing all the time. A builder decided to travel between old Earth's south and north poles at high speed. She left a long vapor trail[bb] behind her that was visible for all to see. Normally, these trails are short in length and slow to form, so the speed of movement was compromised as being far beyond whatever aircraft the humans presently have at hand.'

Jason gauged Chris' reactions with a piercing glance and then decided to wrap up the hearing.

'The charges against you are hereby withdrawn. You are asked however to please plan your trips with a bit more thoroughness in future. Your mentor will explain to you how to cancel a previously transmitted flight plan but it should be obvious that designating the <Cancel> option on your menu would have done the trick. I look forward to meeting with you later Chris regarding your duties while with SS23. This council hearing is adjourned.' Without further ado the council members vanished a second time leaving Brian and Chris to look at each other in relief and jubilation. This time Brian and Chris shook hands, lasers or not. Chris realised that his laser

---

camera a peanut-shaped craft was seen having two internal hot spots. An unexplained plume of some sort was emanating from the craft at times.

[bb] A trail of condensed water from an aircraft or rocket at high altitude, seen as a white streak against the sky. Normally these dissipate quickly and are only seen where the object causing them has travelled.

was still disabled but in addition he knew that it was also in safe mode as was Brian's.

The two transported directly from the boardroom after Brian had re-enabled Chris' teleportation and laser capabilities. Brian complimented Chris on coming through a very harrowing experience with the only consequence being a light reprimand that would not appear on his record. A very relieved Chris arrived back in his cubicle and he sank down on his bed. He wondered if his two stern-faced enforcers had been informed about the termination of the council session and envisaged them still waiting outside the boardroom door to no avail. On that silly thought and after a private giggle he realised that these were advanced enforcers, they would know about his trial's details. They were surely long gone. Chris prepared himself for sleep. Induction would be continuing in Persephone on the morrow.

Chapter Eight

(Where Chris Re-Visits His Understanding of Man's Best Friend and Discovers Some Frailties)

'What do you do for recreation around here except for field trips?' asked Chris at the next training session in Persephone.

'There is a large group of us that like enhancing our field trips by indulging in intergalactic geocaching. You might consider other possibilities such as indulging in sport such as the bridge card game. Other colleagues like to play chess,' said Olympus.

Chris was intrigued to discover that the geocaching[cc] sport that he had indulged in on Earth applied at the SS23 integration facility as well but on a far grander scale. He thought back to the fun he had on Earth. He mused on the details. Geocaching is a high-tech treasure hunt that involves the use of a Global Positioning System (GPS) satellite receiver in order to find a hidden 'treasure'. The coordinates of where a cache is hidden are posted on the internet and geocachers physically go to look for the cache (which sounds easy but is surprisingly difficult). Intergalactic geocaching

---

[cc] Visit www.geocaching.com to read about this fascinating sport.

sounded like it would be even more of a challenge. The cache on old Earth mostly took the form of a two-litre ice cream container wrapped in a black plastic garbage bag. A small item or trinket in the cache would be bartered for an item that the geocachers bring along. A logbook in the cache was used to record the visit (finding the cache) as well as posting a log of the find on the Internet. Some caches required solving puzzles such as solving a sudoku in order to determine the cache coordinates. Persons that did not know about the sport or had not taken part in the sport were called geo muggles. The realisation came to Chris that geocaches placed in various planets in the Universe meant that a new term applied to those not in the know, that of intergalactic geomuggles or intgeomuggles.

Chris concluded that the variant at SSTEP must involve visiting many planets in the galaxy instead of just several locations on one planet such as old Earth! Chris resolved to tackle an intergalactic geocache or two in due course. He decided to explore additional recreational possibilities with Olympus.

'What about contact sports such as Rugby?'

'The best way of doing that is by means of your virtual reality programs since our structures are not that conducive to galloping around on a field with others having the same rugged structure such as your own. Serious damage can occur not only to the individuals but also to the environment should lasers and other equipment accidentally come into play.'

Chris pondered about this and again started to feel slightly homesick.

'Surely, it is unhealthy to focus all of your energies on work-related matters without having some form of physical distraction?' queried Chris in a subdued tone of voice.

'OK Chris, you tell me what it is that you enjoyed doing back on Earth and we can see what can be done,' said Olympus.

Chris pondered for a while and then it hit him. He used to enjoy his interaction with animals and in particular the feel of smooth fur when stroking his favourite dog. He remembered the smell of wet dog after a bath with nostalgia and the friendly tail wagging that would greet him on his return home from work every day. He remembered the head that was pressed against his torso with a wistful request to scratch the long furry ears. He spoke up with enthusiasm.

'I miss having a dog,' said Chris.

Olympus looked taken aback for a time and then a spark of enthusiasm lit up in his quad red optics.

'I think I have an idea and this fits in with our standard recruit counselling service,' he said. 'Wait for me, I will be back shortly,' he said before vanishing.

Chris settled himself on a chair and thought back to his romps through the countryside with butch his bullmastiff. Butch loved chasing sticks and used to whine when Chris and his friends climbed into their tree house. Come to think of it, Chris had not seen any trees in SS23. He was busy comparing SS23 to what he was used to seeing and experiencing on Earth when Olympus returned. Olympus was in the company of a strange contraption and Chris could not stop staring at it in wonder. A short four-legged mechanical marvel was staring at Chris with dual red optics and was tentatively moving a mechanical extension at its rear from side to side. Chris did not miss the similarity to a dog's tail. The quadruped was a nondescript shade of grey and metallic fangs were visible from a mouth that was slightly parted. A lolling appendage between the fangs could only be an approximation for a tongue.

'Chuck me farley,' exclaimed Chris, 'A mechanical dog!'

'Who are you calling a mechanical dog you robot,' growled the apparition and its tail was raised in the air like a scorpion's sting.

Chris burbled for a while; Olympus looked on with an amused glint in his quad optics. 'Let me introduce you to Fido,' he said.

'Hey!' exclaimed the quadruped. 'That is spelt Phydeau!'

Chris burbled some more, realising that not only could the mechanical wonder hear and speak but could visualise the text being used to generate the associated speech by the person speaking. He stared at Phydeau with his metaphorical mouth hanging open.

'Cat got your tongue tin head?' questioned Phydeau with an amused glint in his optics.

Olympus interrupted the long-drawn-out silence by explaining that Phydeau was the SS23 integration centre mascot and psychological consultant. Brian asked what the mascot's duties were and to whom Phydeau belonged. Phydeau interjected with an indignant tone of voice by saying that he didn't belong to anyone, thank you very much. Olympus explained that Phydeau acted as a companion and counsellor to newcomers, helping them to adjust to SS23 life.

'A counsellor?' questioned Chris.

'Phydeau actually was a highly qualified clinical psychologist back on old Earth' explained Olympus. 'He had some social debts to pay and the galactic council decided to make use of Phydeau's talents by providing him with a special form.'

Chris decided to keep his mouth shut and received a congratulatory dual red glance from the quadruped. It was obvious that Phydeau did not suffer fools gladly and was also a bit touchy about his past.

'So Tin Heads,' growled Phydeau at Chris and Peter, 'Have you guys got used to not having your torty[dd] yet? And how do you two flat-chested ladies feel?'

The two female builders were obviously embarrassed by that question and pretended to not have heard it. The male builders looked sheepishly at each other, also embarrassed but silently daring each other to say something. Detecting a delicate situation, Olympus quietly moved to the front of the class to leave the trainees to their discussion with the councillor.

Chris finally looked at Phydeau with a bemused and slightly shocked expression due to the forthrightness of the question before replying in the negative, as did Peter. Phydeau looked at both of them with a disbelieving glint in his optics while the ladies kept their embarrassed silence. Chris finally admitted to missing his third leg and mentioned that the loss was one of the first things he complained to Brian about. Phydeau asked what it was that Brian specifically missed and Brian admitted to mourning the loss of the capability to have sex the most. The peeing part (except for the fun in trying to drown mosquitoes and flies in urinals, trying to pee the

---

[dd] Some people in South Africa refer to male genitalia in this fashion.

furthest, or in writing one's name on a wall in pee) was not really the issue. Phydeau nodded his head in sympathy and requested that Chris follow him and he trotted off down the corridor. With an apology to Olympus and the other three trainees, Chris started off after the clattering canine, wondering what lay in store for him, what it was that Phydeau had in mind. Chris heard Olympus concluding the day's session in the background as the duo exited Persephone.

It shortly became obvious that Phydeau was leading the way to Chris' cubicle and as they drew close the door opened without any command from Chris, much to his surprise. Phydeau observed Chris' surprise and growled that as mascot and councillor he had the run of the place since he often had to minister to the needs of builders in distress. That comment caused Chris to wonder about how much of a utopia the SS23 facility really was. Phydeau trotted over to the cubicle computer terminal above the bed and plugged himself in, requesting Chris to do likewise. Chris observed silently as Phydeau accessed several new menus that Chris had not discovered to date. Suddenly, Chris felt himself to be in a totally different environment and he realised that Phydeau must have activated some form of virtual reality program. Chris no longer saw his cubicle or Phydeau and suddenly became aware of a beautiful scantily clad woman walking towards him. He moved towards her and then nature as it was on Earth took its course.

The orgasm was imminently satisfying and brought him to the realisation that the whole scene had played out, as it would have happened on Earth, with both parties having human form. The scene and the female faded from view and

123

Chris realised he was back in his cubicle once again since the virtual reality program had terminated.

'Now don't do too much of that,' growled Phydeau, 'or you won't be able to do your work.' Chris stared at him in wonder.

'What about the prime reason for intimacy being that of species sustainability in the context of us builders?' asked Chris.

'We are recording a lot of individuals on old Earth', said Phydeau smugly. 'If you have enough credits and you would like to have an additional junior builder as a part of a union with your chosen builder partner, a shell could be built for you and your chosen data record could be transferred. Think of it of being able to choose your child when you want to, a privilege that few humans have on old Earth. An instant family if you like. That would also help to stabilise you and your partner's mental states.'

'Are your middle names Sigmund Freud?' Chris asked.

'No, not quite, but it is my task to help newcomers adjust to the new way of doing things around here and in my present form I can help both sexes without too much embarrassment' quipped the canine. 'Now if you excuse me, I have to leave to speak with the rest of your trainee group and provide some training just like I have done for you. Incidentally now that you know what to do you can do so with anyone of your choice that is prepared to engage the intimate dual communication port protocols with you,' cackled Phydeau with a wicked glint in his eye before he vanished.

Chris added an item to his to-do list to spend more time socializing, Hermien guiltily came to mind as someone that he would like to spend more time with.

Chris stood looking at the spot where the canned canine had stood for some time before retiring for the night. His last thought before blackness descended was the comical thought that he had just technically engaged in sex with a dog.

Chapter Nine

(Socialising and Administration)

The induction training that had continued after the re-tabling of the service contracts had clearly stipulated adherence to all of the prime directives. This adherence included the requirement for secrecy that was effectively an agreement not to divulge SS23 activities, seeding specifics or build standards, to the dark teams or to seedlings. The other three trainees were somewhat still in awe of Chris after he told them of his Cassini experience and the resulting appearance in front of the SS23 facility CEO, the SS23 management committee; followed by the disciplinary hearing. Chris could see that they were starting to think of him as being somewhat jinxed. Everyone was very curious to hear what the galactic council looked like and they were a little disappointed to hear that Jason and his management team mostly looked just like the rest of them. At that point a chime interrupted the proceedings and several builders appeared in the Persephone training centre.

Chris gave the visitor's leader one glance and he knew that Jason had come to visit them along with some of his senior builders. Chris was therefore not surprised when Olympus introduced Jason to the rest of the trainees, along with a builder entitled the prime designer. Chris derived some private pleasure from observing the subdued reactions from the rest of the trainees, especially when Jason recognised him. Jason welcomed them to the facility and after fixing each with a piercing red quad glance hoped that they would enjoy their stay at SS23. After only a few minutes Jason left with his senior team and Olympus explained that time was a precious commodity that the council and SSTEP had little of. Time was always wasting.

After the training for the day the team decided to continue with getting to know each other and decided to convene in Chris' cubicle. Chris wanted to offer everyone something to drink before he realised that they no longer needed to drink and he didn't have a refrigerator or any contents in any case. There was an awkward silence while Chris pondered what to do and what to say. Then a sudden thought struck him.

'You know there are four of us so why don't we play some bridge like Olympus mentioned we could do?' asked Chris.

There was a short silence while the rest of the trainees deliberated on this and then Peter piped up to say that he did not know how to play bridge. Hermien and Mavis followed by saying the same thing and Chris was nonplussed to discover that he was the only bridge player. He deliberated awhile and then found he could remember an acol system bridge summary in perfect detail. He had written that in days gone by for his bridge partner and himself back on old Earth. He was further delighted to find that he could almost immediately generate a digital document to capture the remembered summary and then upload the result to his three colleagues in seconds. There was a silence while everyone digested the contents of the file.

A lot of discussion and questions resulted until Peter joyously piped up by saying that he now understood the bridge dual process of bidding followed by trying to make an agreed-to contract. Peter's enthusiasm was catching and then the next obstacle surfaced. There were no playing cards to be had. Chris pondered again and remembered the days when he and his son played computer games on a network. He decided to test the principles based on their newfound capabilities and to everyone's surprise they worked perfectly. A locally established communications network linking the four builders did the job! They had discovered a way to have fun in SS23!

The four of them were effectively networked with their communication abilities. By using graphics on their head-up displays they could each 'see' their cards but not the other players' cards on command. The cards were 'dealt' from a central program that dealt the 52 cards randomly. The four trainee builders dealt and played several hands. Chris was amazed at the speed in which the hands were dealt and played. He was further amazed that each player could remember each card as it was played and there were no arguments as to the score and who had won which bridge trick. The team played several bridge rubbers and then suddenly collectively realised that it was late. Peter and Mavis decided to call it a day and left in a buoyant frame of mind. Hermien and Chris decided to reminisce and share experiences.

Chris told Hermien that he thought she was doing very well with her cubicle design, much to her gratification. Chris decided to share some of his observations and thoughts as regards the two pairs of SSTEP recruits. He was keen to compare his experiences to Hermien's.

128

'No offence intended, how have you coped with er, your missing body parts?' Chris asked tentatively.

'No offence taken. I was totally unprepared for the way that I arrived here at SS23. Our car crash was horrible. One instant I was driving the family car with my husband and our two children as passengers and the next we had a head-on collision with an incoming car that I couldn't avoid. My side of the car was hit first and I was killed instantly. The next instant after a nasty jarring feeling I found myself looking up at a grey featureless ceiling, amazed that I could do that. Then this scary mechanical monster appeared in my field of view and I was scared out of my wits. It took me some time to accept that apparition as my SSTEP mentor. Angela told me after a time that the rest of my family luckily survived the car accident.' Hermien paused and Chris could see that the recollection of her ordeal was still very painful to her, although knowing that the rest of her family was ok was some measure of solace.

'Once I was feeling a little calmer and with my mentor Angela answering several of my panic-filled questions, I started checking myself to see if I was all right. It was then that I discovered that my form had been totally transformed into what I now know to be that of a builder. My initial reaction was horror. I was convinced that I had been abducted, cut into pieces and replaced with horrible mechanical parts. I didn't want to be a cyborg! I wanted to be back home!' Hermien paused again and Chris could tell that her feeling of loss and sadness were still very much with her. Hermien continued after a time.

'I realised that I didn't have any hair, my face was gone as were my breasts and vagina. I was devastated. It took

Angela some time to calm me down and I soon realised that I was incapable of crying. Screaming didn't seem to make any difference either.' Chris remembered that he had reacted similarly on being reanimated so he could strongly sympathise with Hermien.

'I found that I didn't have anything like the clothing that I was used to wearing on old Earth. In fact, I was wearing no clothes, just this grey featureless exterior was in evidence. It took me a considerable amount of time to realise that I didn't need to eat, visit the toilet, change clothing or to put on makeup. Angela helped me to understand that I had other capabilities that compensated for the losses that I had suffered. Experimenting with my new capabilities and interacting with by cubicle helped me to overcome some of the sadness due to what I have lost. Our induction process in Persephone and a visit by Phydeau further accentuated the gains that I have experienced due to becoming a builder. Knowing that there were three other recruits having similar experiences to mine helped a great deal. Also knowing that we have a responsible task to perform, meaning that I have been given a second chance at this entire sentience thing, has also helped a lot.' Hermien absentmindedly rubbed her domed grey head with one of her talons. Chris interjected.

'Have you noticed that there is a predefined gender as regards our two pairs, namely two men and two women?' probed Chris.

'Yes, I have. I suspect that we were all chosen with this specific combination in mind. Picking an even number is maybe their attempt to keep us sane and balanced?' theorised Hermien.

130

'That does make sense. I have also been wondering if we are being continuously monitored, but maybe I am being too paranoid. I guess that senior builders can access our state and recordings at any time, given that we have a new set of health monitoring sub-systems that form part of our build standard. We owe SSTEP a lot of credits so I guess we cannot blame them for monitoring the state of their investments. I wonder if we will need to sit for exams and receive some form of certification as builders before they let us loose on testing seeding SS23? Say, what did you think of Phydeau's visit?'

'As I said, she consoled me a lot as regards the loss of my family. I feel a lot more settled now,' confided Hermien.

'What you say is interesting. I had the impression that Phydeau was male when he/she visited me. I guess that gender is a role that Phydeau can select at will, given her history and her psychoanalyst function in SSTEP. Her capability is sure a lot easier than gender swopping as we have seen on old Earth. Did Phydeau also connect you directly to your cubicle with him, sorry her, as she did with me?' enquired Chris shyly.

Hermien paused before answering and Chris detected that she was feeling a little embarrassed.

'Yes, she did. I was given a sex education lecture and experience that was out of this world,' confessed Hermien.

Chris could not resist the urge to suggest that they try a dual connection to Hermien's cubicle. Much to his relief Hermien did not take offense. She chalked up the process as being part of understanding how their new forms and capabilities functioned.

After an immensely satisfying 3D simulated intimate interlude and fond farewell, Chris retired to his cubicle.

On arriving at his cubicle, he wondered if it was possible to share one cubicle with two people. Was there something like marriage between consenting builders? He parked that thought and decided to configure his exterior form for tomorrow's lecture in Persephone. He was satisfied with the resulting simulated informal looking open-necked shirt and jeans. He felt that he could overcome this challenge of a new existence, he was stepping in the correct direction! His sleep was deep and dreamless.

Chapter Ten

(Where Chris Re-Visits
His Understanding of 'Testing')

'You mean that all of the reproductive functions are programmed into the human seeding BP?' asked Chris uncertainly.

'Yes, and the same applies to all aspects of any seeding and sub-seeding,' answered Brian with a patient air. 'One has to automate several processes including functions such as heartbeat and respiration in each seedling's BP. Consider the basic functions involved and you will see that it is really quite simple. There are sets of basic rules that apply to all existence. For human beings an oocyte[ee] has to be brought into contact with spermatozoa[ff] in order to achieve the fertilised state. That is however not enough on its own. The combination has to be transported to the uterus' inner wall, the endometrium, in order to obtain a site conducive to cell division and macro growth. This new state is called the pregnant state.

[ee] An oocyte is an ovum, a female egg.

[ff] Sperm is mixed in with all of that unmentionable white stuff. Contrary to belief sperm is not white.

All of these various states inclusive of the transitions between states can be thought of as being a state machine. The state machine is built into each human's BP and each state change reacts upon triggers such as the combination of the oocyte with the spermatozoa and the presence of catalysts and enzymes. That is the normal flow of the process and similarly software engineers on your old Earth often design state machines in this manner. Remember your training as an engineer as regards to 'what can go wrong, go wrong'. Half the job is to get a process working and the other half of the effort has to be directed into getting the process working reliably and even succeeding under conditions of partial system or sub-system failure. What would you expect to be some of the reversionary modes[gg] that are associated with the reproductive process in humans?' asked Brian.

Chris thought about it and then realised what Brian meant.

'If the combination does not reach the endometrium and lodge there in a viable state then the body should reject the union.'

'What does that mean in basic human terms?' asked Brian impatiently.

'Well, the human female miscarriages,' answered Chris.

'Exactly,' answered Brain in an approving tone. 'What happens if the fertilised state is not reached? He asked.

'Well, the menstruation process kicks in and the process repeats,' said Chris.

[gg] A reversionary mode relates to a situation where the unexpected happens that has to be dealt with reliably by a special mode designed to counter the unexpected event.

'Well done,' approved Brian. 'Remember that you will have to test each of the states of the SS23 seeding reproductive functions and test each of the species' reversionary modes. Testing involves investigating mission success, that is confirming the long-term species survival even under adverse circumstances or partial mission failure conditions. Now, let us discuss your test equipment and the integration and test platform that you will use to verify the BP programming,' said Brian.

'What do you mean?' asked Chris helplessly.

Brian again explained that a planet very similar to Earth (but tens of light years away from old Earth as well as far away from the SS23 facility) was one of the chosen sites. A site identified to introduce a prototype of the latest SS23 build standard before finally introducing the seeding to planet 23. The intention was to create a superior species that was less likely to self-extinction. A seeding less likely to destroy the environment to the detriment of its long-term survival. Human beings on the old Earth were much too prone to enjoying life and not considering the impact on their environment and the survival of their children. Admittedly, the human BP had been crafted such that the enjoyment of life made the hardships of life tolerable to the extent that the species did not want to self-terminate. The key lay in improving the species' BP such that there was a lot more tolerance to change. In addition, a lot more appreciation for the environment without destroying initiative, positive curiosity and the evolutionary process was required. Brian went on to describe the manner in which Chris was expected to obtain field test data in order to verify that the improved basic species programming (the now so-called super BP) was effective.

'Do you remember the times that you squashed those solitary fruit flies in the various toilets that you visited inclusive of those mosquitoes at night?' asked Brian.

'Now that you mention it yes,' replied Chris.

'Didn't you think that it was strange that there was only one of the fruit flies visible at a time in your toilet at home and at work and that it was very easy to squish them?' queried Brian.

'Now that you mention it you have a point,' said Chris.

'Seeing as I am doing a lot of mentioning,' said Brian caustically. 'Did you ever think that you were being monitored and that the output of the fruit fly sensor array was being transmitted to integration centre SS23 in real time for storage so we could get your shell database ready for your arrival?' asked Brian.

Chris's head spun and he could not think of anything to burble about other than to want to answer in the negative.

'Some fruit flies, moths and even mosquitoes were equipped with miniature sensors and data transmission links. The mosquitoes took blood samples and the moths provided night-time video surveillance since the fruit flies could only handle daylight conditions,' said Brian smugly. 'The drawback was that the insect surveillance team was slow and could not always avoid your sadistic attacks. They were encumbered with the mass of the special equipment that was monitoring you and slowing them down.'

'Those darn mosquitoes messed up my sleep and what about malaria?' asked Chris indignantly.

'We tried to introduce a means of testing metabolisms without introducing a change to the test subject's environment but that is not as easy to do as you will discover. The malaria part is a dark team adaptation that we could do nothing about. We were able to modify the malaria parasite so that it was only active at low altitudes (before the dark team mutated it further into super malaria) but we could not force humans to move onto higher ground, even the so-called flood could not do that. The dark teams used our test equipment to massacre millions of seedling test cases and we are still plotting our revenge in secret, although the galactic council is not chuffed with the idea of revenge and frowns upon the concept in public. On the Highveld in South Africa, you were mostly not at risk for malaria and in any case, we did not use Anopheles mosquitoes.'

'Aren't we using the human species as guinea pigs in order to test the newer designs? Are we becoming the equivalent of that Nazi Doctor?' asked Chris horrified at the thought.

'I guess you could think of it that way but we do not. Remember we are helping to ensure the species long-term survival and where we can do so in a modified and improved form. Our intentions are altruistic and not self-directed. We need to capture specific individual memories in order to ensure the continuation of the master builders and their seedings. We are very proud of our results to date,' said Brian fervently.

Chris decided to change the subject and to test to what extent he could stretch the self-determination rule.

'What chances are there of my being able to view my family? I want to see how they are doing. I would love to tell them that I am all right and to make sure that they are coping.'

'Seeing them might be possible within the rules as long as they do not know that you are doing so but are you really sure you want to do that? Think of the trauma that you will experience if you witness their grief shortly after your death.

They will move on you know. How will you feel if your wife marries again?'

Chris pondered what Brian had said after a stab of jealousy of imagining his wife with another man and then he wondered what 'within the rules' meant and he asked Brian what the rules were.

'If your family decides to meet with some of the unique people on Earth that have been gifted with the ability to subliminally tie into our communications network then you might be able to pass on a subtle message without compromising our master plan and facilities such as SS23. The problem is that there are several charlatans on Earth that pretend to have a psychic capability and they give the rest that do have a genuine capability a bad name. People in general do not believe that only some people can have capabilities of communicating beyond the grave. A fear of 'ghosts' has also been pre-programmed into your old Earth seeding BP. The rules state that your family has to take the lead if they want to communicate, you cannot do so from here.'

'What does that mean,' asked Chris.

'One of your family members has to go to a gifted person and ask that a contact be established. If they do not do so then you cannot establish a contact from here unless a family member is being recorded and the person is in danger. Even then you need special permission from the galactic council.'

'How do I know if any family member has contacted a psychic on Earth?'

'We could routinely scan the whereabouts of all of the known true psychics that have the capability programmed into their BP relative to the position of various family members associated with our builders. Remember that you will have to pay for the continuation of any psychic scan and you are deep in hock right now already due to receiving your new form and gallivanting to unauthorised places like Saturn'.

Chris pondered and then declared, 'I would like the scan to continue in my case,' he said.

'Done,' declared Brian. 'You will be informed from this time onwards as long as you continue to subscribe to the service if any of your family members opt to contact a viable medium. You can then decide if you want to communicate with that medium if a séance is initiated on Earth. You will be billed accordingly.' Concluded Brian.

After a pregnant silence Brian spoke again.

'It is time that you visit a SS23 seeding test equipment prototype to appreciate a part of the task that the galactic council has given you,' said Brian earnestly. 'Come with me,' he instructed before trundling off down the corridor.

Chris followed in his wake experiencing a mixture of trepidation and expectation.

Their trip led to a green door that Chris had not seen before some distance beyond the Persephone training centre. The door was marked with the red text 'Integration Laboratory SS23'.

There was a lengthy delay that Chris wondered about and then Brian explained that he was invoking security protocols that would allow Chris access to the Laboratory in the future. The door slid open and Chris and Brian silently entered the grey interior. There before them stood a wheeled contraption that could only be a form of aircraft.

'A UAV!' burbled Chris with excitement.

'Let me introduce you to SS23 flight surveillance system issue E although I believe you have met,' said Brian with a sly glance at Chris.

'Hi Chris,' said Issue E after turning his payload sensor array in Chris' direction.

Chris managed to splutter an incredulous greeting followed by the timorous question as to when they had met.

'OK it is true that I didn't quite look like this when last we met,' intoned Issue E.

'But think about test pilots and tell me what name comes to mind when I remind you of the many hours that we spent together at our flight test range on Earth.'

Chris pondered end then he spoke up with a sudden realisation based upon inflections in Issue E's speech.

'Sherbet!' he exclaimed. 'Is that you Charles?' he asked with sudden realisation.

Charles answered in the affirmative and Chris went on a nostalgic trip where he remembered the days that he was a UAV system engineer and Charles was their chief test pilot. He remembered their trials and tribulations while they battled with UAV engine, communications link and avionics problems. He was gladdened to again meet a professional friend although in very strange circumstances. He walked over to Charles and then felt awkward in being unable to shake hands since there were none to be seen on the smooth grey exterior of UAV with its specially adapted sentient autopilot, never mind the laser concerns.

'Issue E is under development as an advanced variant of flight test support equipment and his ground-testing integration phase is almost complete,' said Brian. 'He will be used by our SS23 team to clandestinely monitor how the SS23 seeding and other seedings are progressing for long periods of time. He is only a small part of the full range of the test equipment that we need to establish and also test, to make sure that it complies with our sentient species testing needs. This design is a similar approach to one where we designed the insect surveillance and test teams on your Earth but on a much grander scale,' explained Brian.

'Let's take a further trip into this laboratory, I wish to show you some testing that is in process right now as regards some SS23 sub-systems. You can speak with Issue E again on our way out,' said Brian, belaying any further questions.

The duo trundled down the corridor and came to a door marked with the text 'Sub-system Testing'. After another delay while security protocols were updated, the door irised open and Chris followed Brian into the test area. Chris noted benches festooned with instruments, wiring, tubes and associated equipment that could only be classified as integration bench set-ups. There were many benches in sight, Brian stopped at the first one and Chris curiously moved closer to inspect it.

'What you see before you is the re-designed heart sub-system test bench for the SS23 seeding,' said Brian. The heart that is under test is essentially a pump. That tank with the blue fluid on the left is the simulated blood that is being circulated through the heart. The tank has an output tube going to the heart and an input tube collecting the sim-blood flow from the heart. The controller in the middle is temporarily generating the heart's electrical command impulses as to how to beat and also monitors the status reports coming from the heart via nerve pathways. The four heart chambers, the left and right atrium and the right and left ventricle, have to be stimulated in a fashion that replicate the SS23 mission profile. Eventually, parts of the controller will be embedded in the heart so as to allow the heart pumping function to continue independently. A long-term endurance test is under process. The heart-under-test is presently being intentionally over-stressed so as to simulate a long-term mission in the seeding's target body and to confirm that the overall design meets the designer's specifications.'

'Where did you get a heart to test and how do you know what blood flow rate and electrical signals are required in order for the heart muscles to contract and to pump blood efficiently?' asked Chris.

'The heart was constructed using tridy printing in accordance with the heart's design as held in the configuration management[hh] department. CM provided the correct Tri-D cube with the heart's design after ensuring that the correct heart's build standard was being provided. CM's job is to ensure that the heart-under-test is correct as per the latest SS23 system specification. As regards all of the heart's interfaces, CM also provides the test engineers with the

---

[hh] CM for short.

correct interface control document [ii] that specifies each electrical and other interface performance in full detail.'

Chris stood mesmerised, watching the four heart chambers pumping away furiously while the controller's screen showed the heart's parameters, plots of the electrical signal commands and status indicators including blood flowrate and the heart's beats per second. Brian interrupted Chris' thoughts after a time.

'Let's take a quick trip around this lab, to look at some of the other subsystems that are under test,' said Brian.

They trundled from station to station. Brian pointed out the skeletal subsystem test bench, the liver test bench and the brain test bench amongst others, before suggesting that enough was enough for today.

All that Chris could do was to again shake his head in disbelief. He was stimulated to remember many of his hundreds of hours of shared experiences with testing teams back in the good old days on old Earth. Brian suggested that they spend some time with Charles and they wandered over to the laboratory where Charles was surrounded by various pieces of what was obviously integration test equipment. Chris realised that this would be the first time that he would work with a sentient UAV!

'Charles, it is amazing to see you in that form and also me in this Builder garb, said Chris. Tell me, what makes your form different to mine come to think of it?'

'Well old chap, you are more suited to ground operations and I have been designed for long-range airborne applications. I have several large multi-spectral sensors

---

[ii] ICD for short.

capable of monitoring objects that are very far away. Of necessity I look a lot like an airborne UAV on Earth since I need large pylons to carry my sensor pods.

My optics need long lenses with large apertures so I can obtain decent surveillance images and videos. I might look like a UAV similar to those that you and I are used to but I do have several system upgrades that our UAV systems on Earth do not have,' stated Charles.

'What are those,' asked Chris curiously while Brian listened passively.

'Well, you and I know that seventy percent of any traditional unarmed surveillance unmanned autonomous system[ii] consists of sub-systems that are situated on the ground. The aircraft with its sensor payload is only thirty percent of the whole UAS. Most of the system real estate consists of the ground station with its operators. Normally there are three operators in a ground station, the pilot flying the UAV, the operator controlling the UAV payloads or cameras and then a third operator managing the radio link between the UAV and the ground station. Other support staff are required to perform UAS missions. Technicians are required to prepare the aircraft and the ground station for a mission. An external pilot works along with the pilot inside the ground control station. The external pilot handles the take-

---

[ii] The acronym UAS describes an entire surveillance system. A UAV (the aircraft) is part of a UAS. The ground station acronym is GCS for Ground Control Station, the GCS forms a major part of a UAS and the system operators each have a workstation inside the GCS.

off and landing mission phases while the GCS[kk] pilot handles that part of the mission while the UAV is out of sight of the GCS. Ground support equipment like trolleys, spares, fuel, first-line test equipment, generators and the like add to the ground-based total as do factory facilities, airports with their runways and flight-testing sites. In my case I am the sole operator, I can perform the entire mission unaided and I do not need technicians to be on call. My built-in fault diagnosis systems do not require associated ground station electronics and hardware. I also have a much wider operational footprint than a conventional UAV,' reiterated Charles smugly.

'What can you do that normal UAV systems like those that we worked on cannot do?' asked Chris.

'Ground stations need to communicate with their UAV using line-of-sight radio communications channels since few UAS of the class that we worked on have access to satellites. The further away the UAV is from its GCS, the higher it has to fly due to the curvature of the Earth. The higher the UAV needs to fly, the worse the resolution of the video and the still image of the target area. The fixed-wing UAV variants that you and I tested need to keep flying forwards such that air over their wings generates lift. In my case I do not need air to keep me aloft. Just like you I can hover and I am not bound to having to communicate with a ground station, my range between SSTEP and where I obtain sensor data is not bound by distance. I can hover above a target area at any height. It also does not take me of the order of tens of minutes to climb to an operational altitude before actually performing a

---

[kk] The Ground Control Station is the control centre that manages UAV flight, views and records the UAV payload surveillance data.

mission. I can teleport to where I need to be in a short interval of time. I do not need to refuel.

The greatest advantage is that there is no need for a radio link between the cameras and me as the operator. Radio links are prone to degrading surveillance images and are subject to being jammed. There is no need to have two pilots, other operators or support technicians. I do have a subliminal communication channel just like you do so I can also relay what I observe to SSTEP in real time or record it and play it back when I return from a surveillance mission. There is a large saving as regards training. No UAS operators are required. In my case I am a qualified pilot as you know so I perform the entire mission with ease'.

'We are actually lucky to be speaking with Charles at this time,' Brian told Chris. 'His final acceptance test has checked out fully so the two of us are now going to witness Charles's first flight test.'

'Just like that?' intoned Chris. 'I am used to having weeks of preparation, lots of paperwork that needed approval from the flight safety board, budgeting and cost cutting exercises, arguments over who should attend the test and organising high profile rubbernecks[ll]. Then managing the logistics such as GCS generators, fuel, food and booking the flight test site. Then there was the need to coordinate a chase plane[mm] and to

---

[ll] Rubbernecks are visitors to a flight test site. They are called that since they are continually turning their heads around to view the system deployment, curiously inspect everything and ask a thousand questions.

[mm] Chase planes are typically manned Cessna or other type of aircraft that would observe what the UAV is doing in case of any

train and brief the team as to emergency procedures in case there was any system malfunction. The pilots had to practise the flight beforehand using the system simulator on the software avionics bench inclusive of pilot reactions to simulated system failures,' burbled Chris.

'Charles' advanced technology and also the fact that he is sentient obviates the need for most of what you have listed. Many of his sub-systems are shared with our builder designs and have been subjected to extensive qualification testing. The airspace around SSTEP is reserved for our total use. Should any UAV onboard failure occur, Charles is right there and will take the necessary emergency action. There is no need for any other intervention by system operators in the GCS since he is managing the entire flight on his own. There is no need to test and calibrate him extensively since his readiness state is known at all times just like the rest of us builders, he has built-in diagnostic and test health monitoring sub-systems,' explained Brian. At that time, they felt honoured to be joined by their instructor Olympus who teleported into the laboratory.

Olympus arranged for the three builders to teleport out of the integration lab to a featureless area outside the SSTEP integration laboratory where Charles started to execute his pre-flight checklist. Chris found it strange to not see any GCS nearby and particularly noted that there was no external pilot to be seen, no first-line test equipment and no technicians. There was also no runway in sight. Chris felt out of sorts, this flight test was nothing like what he was used to witnessing!

---

system malfunction and to inform ground search teams should the UAV not properly return to base.

Charles indicated that he would transport vertically to an altitude of three hundred metres, hover for a time and then teleport to a location one kilometre to the north at a height of one kilometre. Once there he would engage his long-range colour sensors and record a 360-degree video of the area surrounding SSTEP. Then he would switch to his infrared sensors to repeat the video scan before returning to his starting point with the other two builders. Charles stated that his subliminal communication channel would be active at all times such that Chris, Brian and Olympus could monitor exactly the same view as would be witnessed and as recorded by him.'

This recording would be appended to a report that Charles would produce after the test and the report would be transferred to CM[nn] to certify that Charles was ready for duty. With that and no further decorum Charles vanished and could be seen hovering above his two colleagues. Chris mused and missed attending a protracted pre-flight briefing, the interaction with GCS operators, interaction with an air traffic controller and the interactions with an external pilot that Chris was used to experiencing as a standard operating procedure. There was no take-off as such. The traditional square flight pattern that was routinely used to confirm system preparedness prior to leaving the GCS in order to perform a mission was also not performed. This mission process was certainly greatly simplified and rapid relative to what Chris was used to! Their subliminal communication channel provided an image of the SSTEP buildings and the three

---

[nn] Configuration Management is the organisation that manages build data and records pertaining to test results.

builders standing next to them as relayed by Charles. Charles vanished from the sky to reappear at the predefined distant location and the builders monitored Charles's colour video of the first 360-degree scan. There was nothing to be seen in the cloudless sky. Only the data superimposed on the video changed to reflect that the scan was actually in progress.

Charles switched to his infrared camera and the second 360-degree scan commenced. The image was once again featureless except for the data overlay. Then suddenly an object was unexpectedly detected at a range of 35 km. Charles stopped his scan at 267 degrees and engaged his auto tracker, as seen by crosshairs that now designated the foreign object. His video display image was now locked on to the unidentified object in real time and the builders realised that the object was stationary at an altitude of around five kilometres above ground level. Olympus spoke up.

'That is a cloaked eavesdropper,' he stated grimly. 'That is why we didn't see anything during the colour video 360-degree scan but the object was picked up in our infrared scan. That can only be a dark team surveillance device trying to spy on our latest build capabilities by monitoring our flight-testing initiatives. They want to steal our technologies to use against us. We were lucky to pick up their presence. Charles, return to base immediately,' instructed Olympus. Charles reappeared close to his two colleagues and the four builders teleported inside the integration facility for a debriefing.

'That flight test was more of a success than I expected, said Olympus. It flushed out an intruder and I have already reported the incident to our enforcers. They will take the necessary action.'

Olympus congratulated Charles and then excused himself. Chris wished Charles all of the best, in the knowledge that they would be interacting a lot in future. He left the integration facility for his cubicle and a bit of rest and recuperation.

Chapter Eleven

(Where Chris Receives Confirmation as to Some of His Limitations)

Chris was surprised to be asleep yet aware of himself dreaming and the intensity of the images flashing before him made him forget that he was sleeping.

He dreamt that he was floating slightly above the surface of a planet that seemed similar to Earth. He realised that his cloaking device was activated and thus he must be on a mission to investigate the progress of a newly seeded sentient species. He spotted a red flowing tide some distance away and mused that the planet must be experiencing volcanic eruptions with the lava making quite an impressive sight. He spotted moving figures ahead of the lavaflow. He moved towards them to evaluate how well the sentient species was handling the environmental challenge provided by the volcano.

He was surprised to see the speed at which the lava was flowing and then saw that the fleeing tribe was teleporting away from the lava in short but sudden spurts. This sentient species was significantly more advanced he realised, than the humans on Earth, although their transportation capability was limited in range. There were similarities to Homo sapiens in that the sentient species had two legs and two arms and a torso to match but the heads were larger and covered by long waist-length black hair. Male and female specimens sported a white shock of hair in the same place at the top right of each elongated head. Obviously, they had greater mental capabilities than humans.

The lava flow puzzled Chris. That lava was flowing uphill! It was also breaking up into independent parts at times that recombined, while relentlessly chasing the fleeing tribe. Chris scanned the horizon but could not find any evidence of smoke to indicate where the volcano was situated. The consistency of the lava and the speed at which it moved just did not gel with lava flows Chris had seen on television on old Earth. The red flow did not seem to indicate any evidence of cooling down, the red colour was pretty consistent with occasional orange and white tinges to be seen.

The tribe ran and alternately teleported towards a huge door set into the side of a mountain. One by one the tribe members disappeared and Chris realised that they were teleporting into the interior of the mountain. After watching the red tide dam up against the door, he decided to teleport inside the mountain himself in order to garner more information about this sentient species and to understand why they were being chased and by what.

He watched the tribe gather together in trepidation and he saw that the door to the mountain refuge was starting to buckle under the onslaught of the flow. The door lost the battle to the attack and disintegrated. The tribe started vanishing again one by one, no doubt fleeing to another place of refuge nearby. The flow was now entirely inside the mountain.

Chris became aware that the flow was moving in his direction despite the fact that he was cloaked! The flow's speed was increasing and definitely targeting his location. Just as he was preparing to teleport away from the planet's surface, the feeling of danger caused him to awaken from his slumber to find that it was almost time to report for his next training session.

Troubled by the dream, he completed his ablutions and decided to walk to Persephone for a change instead of teleporting. Once he got there, he greeted the team and after the normal pleasantries he decided to tell the team about what he had experienced last night.

The trainees listened to Chris' description of his dream with rapt attention. Even Olympus evidenced some wonder and curiosity as Chris described the lava flow. The narrative of the flow attack on Chris that culminated in him waking up prompted Olympus to call the class to order.

'What Chris has detailed serves as a very good introduction to a lesson that I wish to impress upon you and that is to highlight that you are not omnipotent. You can be damaged and you can cease to exist,' stated Olympus with a harsh glint in his quad optics.

'In fact, there are other sentient species in the galaxy that would love to get hold of you and to use you as a part of their evolution and expansion. The dark teams would love to kidnap and subvert you so they can steal our latest technologies. There are several levels to creation from nano level to macro level and many sites where sentient but malevolent species exist that are capable of breaching your security mechanisms inclusive of your cloaking device.'

'What do you mean by the term nano level?' enquired Peter.

'Sentient species can be very small. On Earth you must have seen the tendency to make devices such as cell phones smaller and smaller while adding more and more features. The term 'nanotechnology' relates to a technology where functions are performed by using incredibly small hardware entities, possibly even atoms,' stated Olympus.

'In fact, one of the sentient species that we seeded on a planet nearby was based upon nanotechnology. The species operates by applying cooperation between individual nanites. The nanites interlock, form complex structures and perform complex functions inclusive of finally achieving teleportation capability. We code named that species SS18. Obviously, SS18 is one of the predecessors to SS23. The only thing that I find puzzling is that Chris here knows that they call their lava-like enemies 'the flow', he finished with a piercing glance at Chris.

Silence greeted this revelation until Chris finally burbled a garbled question.

'Do you mean to tell me that my dream of a predatory lava flow reflects reality?' he asked incredulously.

'Yes.' Answered Olympus. 'Now all we need to do is to understand how this could have happened. I want to know how you could have gone with this flow while dreaming in a way that mirrors reality,' quipped Olympus. He was quiet for a time and the students realised that he was silently interacting with other unseen SSTEP team members. He came out of his reverie and addressed the class.

'I have some news from our systems engineering team and this affects all of us in a positive manner. Recent changes

154

to our build standard improved our subliminal multi-spectral communications capabilities in a slightly unexpected but good way. Our receivers and transmitters had their spectrum bandwidth increased for the simple reason that there is a desire to also better cloak our electromagnetic emissions when we converse with each other. Spread spectrum [oo] techniques were employed to hide and also to further encrypt our communications channels in the past. Due to the fact that wider frequency band receivers were designed and implemented, meant that we could also receive unexpected transmissions from sources that we don't normally monitor. Even though he was asleep, our piece of charcoal here was able to pick up the activities taking place on the SS18 planet,' explained Olympus.

'Enough for now. Let's proceed with your induction program. The topic for today is to discuss your upcoming examinations and your subsequent certification as professional builders, that is if you pass and before you get assigned your first formal tasks.'

The trainee builders looked at each other with some bewilderment; no one had expected that there really would be an evaluation before they could continue with their testing tasks.

'You all know that you were chosen as data sources for recording purposes while you were on Earth, so you actually

---

[oo] A spread spectrum radio transmission spreads its data content across a wide band of frequencies. The result looks like background noise to an eavesdropper that doesn't have the encryption key. This allows communication to take place between authorised senders and receivers without being detected.

passed your first screening a long time ago. However, it is now necessary to confirm what roles you will perform here at SSTEP, to ensure that we have a cohesive team. There is no 'I' in 'team'. You have not worked directly with each other up until now, you have experienced traumatic experiences to get here and it is necessary to ensure a high probability of SS23 seeding integration, test and deployment success. There will be written, oral and practical evaluations. Further psychological evaluations will be performed by Phydeau and I have been tasked to provide a recommendation report to our CEO Jason for each one of you,' intoned Olympus.

'This process is a team process, so we will now get each one of you to tell the rest of the team what you believe are your strengths and weaknesses. Phydeau is remotely monitoring your responses. Each of you should indicate where you believe you should best fit in with the SS23 team. Let's start with you Chris.

'My expertise lies in unmanned autonomous system general system engineering[pp] as well as being active in the system integration and test process. I focused most of my energies on ground station design and particularly on software testing along with a team of engineers. I work well in team context although I am not particularly good in handling conflict within a team. I think that initially I would be best

---

[pp] System engineers are responsible for the life-cycle performance of an entire system. This includes generating the system specification and seeing to the establishment of aspects that include technical manuals, training, system safety and reliability. System flight testing, qualification, production support and system maintenance aspects need to be considered.

suited to testing key SS23 seeding sub-assemblies such as the brain and the BP[qq] to confirm if there is a better balance to innovation versus aggression in the seeding, relative to the human seeding,' said Chris.

'That is an excellent summary and it makes sense Chris, given that the SS23 system specification already exists. There already is a master designer acting as our system engineer and that we are presently entering the seeding system level testing phase so you needn't write any specifications just yet. We will talk more about this indue course. Hermien, you are next.'

'I was a microbiologist back home. My duties were to plan and conduct complex research projects, such as improving viral sterilization procedures or developing new drugs to combat infectious diseases. I had to perform laboratory experiments that are used in the diagnosis and treatment of illnesses. I used the CRISPR[π] DNA splicing tool to develop environmental microorganisms and then I would track their development. That involved growing microbe cultures. The research led me to developing new pharmaceutical products, vaccines, medicines and compounds. I also had to collect samples from a variety of

---

[qq] The basic programming is the automatic part of a seeding's makeup, handling all aspects such as fight or flight, eating, breathing and brain rejuvenation while sleeping.

[π] CRISPR gene editing is a genetic engineering technique in molecular biology by which the genomes of living organisms may be modified. This gene-splicing tool enables the manipulation of DNA so as to achieve a modified living entity that functions differently to a starting point entity. The technique allows cutting and splicing DNA segments into a starting point DNA sequence at precise locations.

locations, record, analyse and interpret the resulting data. I believe that I am best suited to evaluating the SS23 seeding at microbial level and confirming that changes to the human DNA being used as a baseline for the seeding performs as desired. I get very irritable if others interrupt me while I am working, I have to stay focused and if I make mistakes the result could be something catastrophic such as causing a virus pandemic.'

'Very good Hermien, it makes sense that you apply your experience to our SS23 goals at microbial level. Peter, it is your turn,' said Olympus.

'I was a project manager[ss] before my car accident in an aerospace company. I generated contracts, negotiated with customers and saw to the signing off on contracts. Once the contract was awarded, I led project planning sessions, coordinated staff and internal resources and managed the project progress, adapting the work flow as it progressed. I ensured that projects met their deadlines and I reported on progress regularly to management. I facilitated relationships with clients and stakeholders. I would work best in project management context here as well, monitoring how we are progressing with the SS23 work. I can handle the reporting aspects to facility management. I am a people's person although I don't suffer fools gladly and that has got me into hot water in the past,' explained Peter ruefully.

[ss] Project managers and system engineers work symbiotically in aerospace companies. System engineers handle the technical aspects relating to a project while project managers handle the financial, scheduling and customer relations aspects.

'Good Peter, listening to you it seems to me that you have found a technical ally in the guise of Chris. I am hoping that the two of you work well together in order to facilitate our work with seeding SS23. Right Mavis, let's hear your story.

'I am an endocrinologist. I specialised in working with the glands that are responsible for producing and releasing hormones into a bloodstream. These hormones are vital because they coordinate bodily processes ranging from metabolism to cell growth. We diagnose and treat diseases such as diabetes and hypothyroidism. We examine patients, study their medical records and provide diagnoses. We provide medical solutions for treating a diverse range of diseases and disorders including osteoporosis, high cholesterol and metabolic disorders. I informed patients about complementary health activities and treatments (relating to appropriate diet and exercise). In order to perform the above I executed physical exams, prepared, trained, gave feedback and taught resident students. I utilise ultrasound-guided biopsies. I also had to be familiar with medical billing procedures and making sure that I procured patient consent when needed under the hospital rules and regulations. I am hoping that I can monitor the hormonal stability of the SS23 seeding and I am further hoping that I will see an improvement in the seedling design to lead to fewer cases of diabetes and other causes of death that have hormonal imbalances as the cause. I too, like Peter and Hermien, am work focused and I hate to be interrupted,' smiled Hermien.

'Very good Mavis and the rest of you. You are confirming our analysis as to what this team's composition should look like. That implies that the four of you should work together with the minimum amount of discord. You surely realise that you are not alone and that there are other teams working on SS23 in parallel with you. There are many experts in several disciplines that make up the total SS23 team. You will meet with them in due course. However, Mavis touched on an important aspect that the rest of you didn't specifically cover. Once you have had sufficient experience you will be required to identify sentient candidates in the galaxy for recording purposes. Then you will mentor them once they have passed on and been integrated into their new form. In other words, you will perform some of the mentoring and training functions that Brian has been performing with Chris. I have been conversing with Phydeau and he is satisfied with our discussion today. So, what I need for all of you to do now, is to generate job description drafts along the lines of what we have discussed and then submit them to me,' Olympus instructed.

The team went into a flurry of activity to discover where the equivalent of a word processor was to be found in their menu system. They found that there was a JD template and they all added to their version thereof accordingly. Everyone submitted the result to Olympus via the subliminal communications channel and he promised to review and provide appropriate feedback tomorrow.

'Ok, that is enough for today, we will convene again tomorrow in Persephone.' Olympus concluded the training session and the team left for their cubicles. Chris dropped in to visit Hermien. They compared JDs before calling it a night.

Chapter Twelve

(Where the Trainees Are Somewhat Disillusioned)

'Good morning,' intoned Olympus. 'I trust that you all had a good rest?'

The recruits all indicated that they were well rested and were raring to go. Hermien could not contain her curiosity and posed a question that she believed all four trainee builders would want answered.

'Is there any feedback as regards our CVs and when can we expect to sit for our exams?'

'Congratulations, all of your CVs have been accepted as they are and have been placed on your central files in approved form,' responded Olympus. 'That means that you are all now SSTEP certified builders. As regards your exams I wish to remind you what you were told when you transferred into your new bodies when you arrived here. Your lives on Earth were recorded for many decades and in the process, you were evaluated and deemed suitable for performing your SSTEP future work. No further evaluation is necessary except for confirming that you agree with the centre's evaluation and that you are happy as regards your chosen speciality field while you are here. The only evaluation that took place after your arrival as regards exams was your interaction with Phydeau. We needed to ensure that you were able to mentally handle your transition into your new form and that you will all function well together as a team. I was teasing you about the possibility of exams,' smiled Olympus with a humorous glint to his quad optics.

'Now I am certain that you are all keen to hear where you will be placed in SSTEP as regards the other teams and how you will proceed with your detailed work. SS23 seedlings do need to be tested extensively to ensure their long-term survival as a new species. However, I was contacted last night by Rupert the galactic council chairperson. There has been a sudden change in plan. He will be joining us in a moment,' quipped Olympus.

The four trainees gaped at each other owlishly after hearing this revelation and they wondered what this was all about. They did not have long to wait. A chime sounded and Rupert stood before them; no doubt having teleported in after conferring with Olympus about the visit arrival time. Something very important must be taking place for such a senior person to make the time to visit four new recruits with their instructor. The six builders greeted each other and then the trainees fixed their attention on Rupert in anticipation.

'My apologies for interrupting your SSTEP induction and placement process but a matter of some concern has come to the notice of the galactic council. I need to brief you and then task you for a special mission. This mission is classified secret. I expect all of you to not discuss or disclose what I am about to tell you with anyone or anything outside of this room. In addition, a cloaking field is now in place all around this room in order to prevent the possibility of any eavesdropping

162

while I brief you. I expect you all to suitably encrypt any knowledge that you will store this morning in your data banks. Do you all understand and concur?' Rupert queried.

All of the trainees agreed and Rupert continued.

'I am sure that you are wondering why it is that I have selected this team to be tasked instead of other resources at my disposal. It is quite simple. Our other teams are actively engaged in their tasks and won't be affected by your absence or presence yet. You are new to SSTEP and as such are unlikely to cause a stir should you not be heard from or seen for a time. Let me move on to the background for this tasking. We recently sent Charles on a reconnaissance mission to Earth to see how matters stand with the human seeding and to further confirm his operational readiness for SS23 field trials. While he was there, he detected a cloaked space ship that was busy releasing a plume of some sort of matter into Earth's atmosphere behind it. This is the latest in a string of events that are starting to form a disturbing pattern. Chris recently had an encounter with a team that was attempting to kidnap him, as you all know. Then yesterday Charles detected an object that was monitoring SSTEP from some distance away when we were busy with his maiden flight test. His most recent mission to Earth detected cloaked foreign entities at work on the planet that are busy performing subversive acts. We conclude that there are some malevolent forces at work that seem to be determined to thwart our seeding programs,' Rupert said solemnly.

'I have to provide you with further background information in order for you to understand the context. There is an intergalactic treaty in place that has been honoured by galactic federation member sentient species that are scattered throughout our galaxy. This treaty does not allow interference with Earth's seeding by galactic federation members. I know that you have been told as a matter of policy that Earth was quarantined due to the warlike nature of the human seeding, which is partially true. However, the prime reason for Earth being in isolation is the treaty that was established by the galactic federation after the Great War that took place on Earth in the past,' stated Rupert grimly.

The trainees swopped puzzled glances, wondering what war was being described and why there was this sudden revelation that other sentient species must be more warlike than the trainees had previously been told. Rupert continued.

'We need to discuss some ancient history that happened after this galaxy emerged from its Big Bang. Life as we know it is inherent in the ancient grand design. Matter come into existence in many locations over millions of years based upon the recurring latticework of dark matter[tt] and dark energy[uu]. There is a cycle of perpetuity in the cosmos. Big Bangs occur in a never-ending series and within each of those there are civilisations that emerge to ultimately disappear. All sentient beings originate in several places in the universe in parallel at different times and in a never-ending cycle. We call this the multiverse. It is inevitable that each sentient race will be forced to leave their home planet sooner or later once the resources to sustain life on each planet run out. So, each

---

[tt] Dark Matter can't be seen but it affects other parts of the universe for example by bending light. It consists of 27% of the universe. Normal mass (planets, gas, dust and stars) makes up 5%.

[uu] Dark Energy is forcing standard matter apart and reportedly causing the universe to expand. It consists of 68% of the universe.

sentient race inevitably has to seek other places to live in the universe and that prompts the emergence of the necessary technologies in order to do so. Many seeding programs spring up regularly in parallel. I presume that you trainees have wondered who it was that built us builders?' queried Rupert.

There were nods all round so Rupert continued.

'In this part of our multiverse we had many ancients in different locations that came into being first after the big bang. Several such older civilisations sprang up that eventually were able to conquer faster than light speeds so they could colonise and seed other planets. Several such civilisations sprang up in various constellations. Earth became a planet of interest to several of these constellations due to it having liquid water and a relatively temperate climate. Two of the better-established ancient groups originated from the Pleiades and the Orion constellations. Both of these ancient groups established bases on Earth. Unfortunately, they started encroaching on each other's territory and competing for resources. The Pleiades star cluster inhabitants were masters at DNA definition and manipulation technology. They seeded Earth with an entire ecology from single-celled life all the way up to huge dinosaurs. Some of this ecology started to interfere with the Orion group's resources and settlement. That resulted in some friction between the groups. When that happens self-preservation kicks in and violence tends to result with war becoming inevitable if the issues escalate. Several of the disasters on Earth such as floods and the destruction of cities were actually primarily due to these two groups waging war upon each other[vv]. Such wars included the use of atomic weapons and the use of molecular disrupters that turn flesh into different matter states such as salt, carbon or even basalt. There was one massive aerial conflict in the skies over Earth that resulted in heavy casualties on both sides, inclusive of the loss of motherships on both sides. The seedlings on Earth were the ones that suffered the most. As a result of that, the Intergalactic Treaty was established once a cease fire was negotiated. As a result of the agreement all warring parties had to leave Earth and take all instances of their technology with them. That is where we stand today. The concern is that a party or parties are breaking the treaty.' Rupert paused, confirmed that he had the audience's rapt attention and then continued.

'The other possibility is that an unknown sentient species not part of the galactic federation or one that is not a signatory to the treaty is to blame for the recent increase in tensions. The present belief amongst federation members is that this is the case. That is why we all refer to 'dark teams' since we do not have sufficient knowledge as to whom or what they are. Officially, we are not that concerned as to what they are doing but in reality, we are concerned about their hidden motives and negative impacts upon our seedlings. There is an unconfirmed suspicion that they are shape shifters that can take on the appearance of galactic federation members at will

---

[vv] There are locations on Earth where rock has been vitrified, subjected to extreme heat, but no known human made atomic weapons were ever detonated there. Consider Rajasthan in northwestern India and refer to the Sanskrit epic from India called the Mahabharata.

and by doing so they can infiltrate our societies and seedings. OK, enough for now. That should be sufficient as an introduction as to what it is that you will face during the upcoming mission and why you need to be side tracked from your induction process at this time. I now need to task you specifically in more detail,' he said.

'You need to investigate and determine what it is that the dark teams are introducing into Earth's atmosphere. I will shortly provide you with the exact coordinates of the unknown cloud that we detected. You also need to monitor what it is that they are doing amongst Earth's population and why. There is a World Economic Forum[ww] meeting coming up soon. Given the nature of this meeting and the high-level standing of the attendees, you should eavesdrop on the activities to hear if there is any dark team intelligence to be had. I expect to receive reports on both counts from you within one week. Your reports must be presented to me orally for purposes of secrecy here in Persephone without using our subliminal communications channels. I will see to it that you do not need to log any flight traffic plans with central, that you are empowered to go where you need to go within the confines of your mission. That immunity from red tape should help to disguise your activities and not raise any dark team suspicions. Seeing as this is a special tasking, all reasonable costs will be borne by SSTEP within the mission confines.

[ww] The Forum engages the foremost political, business, cultural and other leaders of society to shape global, regional and industry agendas. Meetings normally take place yearly in January at a ski resort in Switzerland and are by invitation only. The most relevant discussions take place after-hours amongst global leaders.

Depending upon how successful this mission is, you might receive a suitable financial incentive before you are released to your intended SSTEP SS23 work. I will now leave it up to the five of you to plan and execute the mission details and schedule your actions accordingly. Olympus, I wish for you to act as a go-between if I am not available in the week ahead if the away team needs to communicate for whatever reason before we meet again. Are there any questions?'

The trainees and Olympus looked at each other and it was obvious that they felt that they had sufficient detail in order to proceed with mission planning. On that note Rupert left them after confirming the required report-back meeting scheduled for one week's time as being first thing in the morning in Persephone.

'Gosh this means that we have all become special agents! I guess I can help to coordinate our plan, given my background in project management,' Peter proposed. There were no objections, so he continued.

'I suggest that we split up into two teams. Hermien and Mavis should tackle investigating those dark team atmospheric emissions that we were told about. After all, a microbiologist and an endocrinologist should complement each other nicely in that regard. Chris and I will tackle the surveillance aspects related to that alleged interference with the human seeding on Earth. That approach makes sense given the normal symbiotic relationship that exists between a system engineer and a project manager. In that manner team members will get to know each other a lot better. It is without saying that we will be cloaked at all times and that we will avoid making ourselves seen or heard. Let's avoid all contact between our two away teams unless there is an emergency and let's not over complicate our arrangements. Let conditions at each point in time dictate as to where we will go and what we will do until we meet in one week. At least both teams have a starting point from which to conduct our evaluations thanks to Rupert's briefing. I don't think that we need discuss this any further, are you all in agreement?'

The team agreed that they were ready and it was time to depart. The four trainee builders checked their transit menus to discover that flight plans had already been entered for them and were approved. It was only necessary to designate their <Engage> function and Olympus remained in Persephone on his own for a time, before retiring to his cubicle in a pensive mood.

Chapter Thirteen

(Where the Secret Agents Report Back)

'Good morning,' intoned Olympus. 'I trust that you all had a successful mission given that I didn't hear from you at all while you were away?'

'We believe that we were able to obtain the information that Rupert asked for,' said Peter.

'That is good to hear, Rupert is on his way.'

The standard chime sounded and Rupert stood before them. After the normal pleasantries and greetings, Peter informed Rupert that two reports had been prepared. Hermien would present the first report and he, Peter, would present the second. Hermien then started her narrative.

'We teleported to the area above ground where the offending cloud was expected to be but we couldn't find any sign of it. We concluded that it had dissipated due to the passage of time and prevailing atmospheric conditions in particular the wind and maybe sun action. We decided to institute a grid pattern search in the general and remote areas to see if another cloud would make its appearance. After several days of this we were close to giving up when we struck it lucky. We detected a cloaked ship by using our infrared detectors. The ship was initially moving at a leisurely pace and there was nothing to see other than the ship itself. We kept a respectable distance from the ship in order not to be detected and we recorded many 3-D images. Here is a projection of what we saw.'

Hermien projected a 3-D image into the middle of the room for the team to observe. She rotated the image slowly to allow an inspection from all angles. A peanut-shaped craft was exposed, surrounded by its cloaking field. There was evidence that the central part in each peanut segment had a solid core that was obviously distinct from the rest of the structure. The craft was of significant size, around 500 metres in length and 100 metres in height.

'After a time, the craft released a cloud of particles from one end of the peanut. We observed but did not move any closer. The cloud expanded in size, looking somewhat like smoke or mist.' Hermien allowed her recording to move forward in time and the audience could see the cloud expand for themselves. The builders silently watched the cloud expand in size.

'After a time, the craft suddenly left the scene at extremely high speed.' Hermien showed the builders that part of the recording. Now all that there was to be seen was the steadily expanding cloud. Some parts of it were already moving downwards to the city below, no doubt due to the effects of gravity. Some swirling of the cloud particles was evident due to wind action.

'We waited for some time and then we moved close to parts of the cloud. We took some cloud samples then we left the site to a location that we had previously identified as being secure. We performed microscopic examinations of several of the samples. They turned out to be tiny transparent spheres each having different diameters. They varied vastly in size and had sub-particles inside of them. It became evident to us after a while that the spheres were carrying pathogenic payloads. Each sphere's payload consisted of around one thousand sub-particles and there were millions of spheres. We investigated the outer shell of several sphere samples and we found that we could disrupt the shells relatively easily in order to obtain access to the payload contents. Interestingly, we found that the enclosing spheres have a built-in timing mechanism. They can all or individually be triggered by the makers to release their payload at any time. We found the payloads to consist of different viruses, bacteria, fungi and other pathogens likely to detrimentally affect Earth's seeding at all ecology levels, from the simplest to the most complex. We were able to inspect several of the nucleotides[xx] in sample virus DNA structures and we could compare them to our databases. We have many results. We discovered polio viruses as evidenced by their size and as further evidenced by their 8,000 nucleotides. The viruses are slightly larger than 30 nanometres[yy] in diameter. These specific viruses are slightly larger and have more nucleotides than the polio variant that has largely been eradicated on Earth but the basic structure is the same.' We found modified coronavirus samples having

---

[xx] Nucleotides form the basic structural unit of nucleic acids such as DNA. Human haploid genomes have around 3 billion nucleotide base pairs.

[yy] The diameter of a human hair is around 90 micrometers. Three thousand polio viruses stacked side by side would be needed to equate to one human hair's diameter. That is around 10 000 times smaller than a grain of salt.

around 30 000 base pairs[zz] with a size of 100 nanometres. Hermien paused to see if the audience was following her and after noting their rapt attention, she continued.

'We discovered a slightly modified smallpox virus at around 300 nm in size and having around 200,000 nucleotides. There even was a modified Mimivirus [aaa] at around 750 nanometres in size. In all of these cases there is evidence that the viruses are more infectious to the human seeding than previous versions and have a fast-acting stealth characteristic. They mutate rapidly and will therefore be able to defeat human seeding immunities, drugs and vaccines like never before. We found a Candida Auris[bbb] bacteria that is likely to even be more resistant to antibiotics than the superbug version that we know is spreading in hospitals. We found modified tapeworm genomes that are 170 million base pairs in size. The list is endless, we found several thousand pathogen types in the samples that we took.'

'This is incredibly distressing to hear,' Rupert said. 'Let's hear from Peter as regards their observations at the World Economic Forum.' Peter moved to the front of the podium and began presenting the joint report that he and Chris had put together.

[zz] Four nucleotides form two base pairs.

[aaa] A Mimivirus (mimicking microbe virus) is the largest sequenced to date at around 1.2 million base pairs.

[bbb] Candida Auris attacks the central nervous system, kidneys, liver, bones, muscles, joints, spleen and eyes. It presents with other co-morbidities such as diabetes, sepsis, lung diseases and kidney diseases.

'We teleported to a safe distance above the InterContinental Davos [ccc] hotel in Switzerland where we could hover and observe what was happening below. From that height the 'golden egg' architecture made for a stunning view. We scanned the environment and were thankful to not detect any evidence of any cloaked craft in our vicinity or near the Davos Lake. The quiet mountain setting looked peaceful and we could only detect hikers in the woods and some people skiing in the vicinity. The conference delegates had evidently not arrived yet. We inspected the hotel using our penetrative radar with a view to finding spaces where we could hide in various spaces in cloaked form, preferably areas having a high ceiling. We found four conference rooms having 4.5-metre-high ceilings named the seehorns that could handle our cloaked forms. The main seehorn conference locale could hold 430 people so that was a likely venue for any main event. There were seven other locations and a lounge, but they only provided a three-metre space, so we deployed temporary remote monitoring equipment at ceiling height for those and tied them into our subliminal communications network. And then we waited for the conference to begin. We noticed delegates trickling in during the next couple of days and that gave us the opportunity to confirm that all of our equipment was working properly.' Peter paused after having set the scene and moved on to the Davos conference process.

'We monitored the formal greetings and introductions as the conference started. The agenda seemed perfectly innocuous, focusing on world issues such as manufacturing,

---

[ccc] The hotel opened in 2013 to serve as a vacation and business resort in the Grison Alps. The hotel is also called the Alpengold.

investments, global economic interdependence, climate change, global warming, poverty and sickness. There was initially nothing that we could detect during the daily deliberations to suggest dark team interference. Then our remote surveillance equipment in the smaller conference rooms provided us with a lead. There was a mixed group of ten men and women that were meeting regularly after hours in the U-shaped Aster committee room. We focused on what this team was discussing. It became apparent that they were looking at ways to subvert the progress that was being made relating to global advancement by the other convention delegates. By listening carefully, we were able to confirm that they believed the world to be over-populated by a factor of one third and they were dedicated to eradicating large numbers of humans and also reducing population growth firstly to zero and then to a negative growth.' This pronouncement by Peter left the builders dumbfounded. He continued after noting their shocked response.

'The group gloated that they had found a simple yet effective recipe for success. All they needed to do was distribute false information to the masses via social media, debunking truths. Some of the truths that they were working on to undermine were the reality of global warming and the need to vaccinate. By convincing or brainwashing trusting or deliberately misinformed masses of people, these people could be made to simply do nothing! By doing nothing Earth's greenhouse gases would increase until thermal runaway would take place. Fires and the destruction of food sources would then work perfectly well to reduce the population. If people did not vaccinate then they would be more prone to get sick, spread contagion to others and allow viruses to mutate, thereby making pandemics nearly impossible to control. So, by getting populations to do nothing, a simple task for many people especially the lazy, the human seeding on Earth could be eradicated in the shortest possible time. After we gleaned this information, it was time for us to return home to report, so we collected all of our equipment and teleported back to SSTEP.' Peter concluded his report and waited expectantly for Rupert to respond.

'Thank you very much all of you. As a token of appreciation your outstanding debt to central finance will be reduced by five percent. These are extremely disturbing facts that you have presented. I wish you to repeat your presentation to the SS23 central management committee. I have arranged for an immediate emergency meeting, so let us be on our way.' The six builders accordingly teleported to the boardroom. The quartet of trainees found themselves under the scrutiny of the twelve management members, with Jason now sitting in his customary central position and Rupert sitting next to him. He asked Hermien and Peter to repeat their presentations after warning everyone present that the detail under discussion was classified. After the presentations were made, Rupert addressed the committee.

'Given what we have heard, it is obvious that moves are afoot to try to delete the human seeding on Earth. It is doubtful that members of the galactic federation would be behind this, given the thousands of years that the Treaty has withstood the test of time. The most likely explanation is that a group of sentient beings that are not part of the federation wish to make Earth their home, maybe their home planet is under threat such as what we have seen elsewhere in the Universe many times. In any case we will need to confirm who or what is behind this attack on Earth and then we will need to eradicate the threat so as to allow the human seeding to reach maturity in a proper way. So, I call on all committee members to formulate a strategy and an appropriate plan to remedy the threat as soon as possible. Olympus you should also discuss the matter with your trainees and formulate where you can help in the process. I will now go to brief the galactic federation Council using Peter and Hermien's recorded reports. I will reconvene a committee meeting in due course.'

With that Rupert vanished from the room and one by one the rest of the builders did likewise.

Chapter Fourteen

(Where Plans Are Made to Counter the Threat)

'Good morning,' greeted Olympus. 'I trust that all of you have had a chance to think about what happened yesterday and have deliberated amongst yourselves? Before we get on to debating the situation on Earth, I have some news for you of an unprecedented nature. This came to me directly from Rupert last night, the chairperson of the galactic federation council. Our galactic systems engineering team have further analysed the sphere samples that Mavis and Hermien collected over Earth. The sphere shells are even more sophisticated than we originally thought. They include a built-in self-destruct mechanism. That means the makers can decide when to release the payloads, where to release the payloads and could even elect not to activate the spheres by aborting their attack. In addition to that, the team managed to crack the abort command encryption key. We can now also destroy the spheres to prevent wholescale genocide of all seedings on Earth. There is one drawback. We have found that we have to be extremely close to the spheres in order to initiate the self-destruct command. One has to be closer than 100 metres to them in order for the spheres to recognise the encrypted, transmitted command and to accordingly neutralise the threat. There is evidence to suggest that the spheres have been deployed across a significant portion of Earth. We just do not have sufficient craft, motherships and builders to be able to counter the threat rapidly, before the dark team could trigger widespread contagion. Intelligence at our disposal suggests that this action might be weeks or even days away. The council has deliberated the dilemma at length and has decided that they have to elicit the help of the human seedlings as well as mobilising other craft and resources from the galactic federation. It is anticipated that even with our best efforts we will not be able to counter the destruction that will be caused by all of the intact spheres. Help will have to be offered to the Earth seeding populations in order for them to help themselves survive and come to age in the galaxy in a normal manner.' Olympus paused to witness the disbelieving stares from the four trainees.

'Once again, I am afraid that we have to temporarily suspend your deployment to departments within SSTEP. You need to witness the unfolding of the council's contingency plan and the master plan now specifically tailored to preventing the attack on Earth. We need to decide where we as SSTEP and in particular we as a small team of builders will fit in, so as to help counter this attack. Some galactic council contingency plans have been in existence for some time. The council already has a plan as to how to inform the peoples on Earth that they originated from elsewhere in the galaxy. The plan is intended to inform them that they are not alone and in a manner that should not cause mass hysteria and chaos. The first step of that plan will now be implemented by Rupert himself. Rupert will address the United Nations delegates at their upcoming meeting in their General Assembly Hall in a surprise manner that is not on their agenda. As you know, the hall houses up to 1800 delegates from 193 member states. The United Nations was established in 1945 and has a headquarters in New York. The World Health Organisation is one of its subsidiaries and the galactic council will need to enlist their health experts. The UNICEF child emergency fund is expected to be tasked, as will the UN Security Council. The General Assembly Hall is perfect for what Rupert is about to do; it has a high ceiling. The fact that there are around 190 member states present, allows all of them to receive exactly the same message at the same time. Rupert can tap into the hall's audio communications network and what he says will be translated into several Earth languages on his behalf. Our timing for today's meeting is perfect. Rupert is ready right now to proceed with his surprise UN announcement. We will monitor what is said and what happens in real time via our subliminal communications channels.'

Olympus completed his announcement by silently asking the builders to not interject in Rupert's speech to the delegates. He informed the trainee quartet that the UN Secretary General was busy speaking right now, welcoming the delegates to the venue and the sitting of world leaders. Let us listen silently while Rupert speaks using the Hall's audio equipment. He will speak before he reveals himself.

'United Nations Secretary General and delegates. My name is Rupert. I am the chairperson of the galactic federation council. I know it is not the best way to start any presentation by apologising, but I assure you today will be an epic and unprecedented occasion that should be remembered by many of you. I apologise for interrupting your normal proceedings and not having had the opportunity for meeting with you personally before today. Please do not be alarmed. I can assure you that what I intend to present to you today holds great importance to the future of Earth. I know that you cannot view me at this time but I will rectify that shortly. Before I do rectify my rudeness by interrupting your meeting, I need to ask your security team to not shoot at me when they see me. That can be quite uncomfortable and potentially could cause harm to you as our honourable delegates, should the shooters' shaking hands cause them to miss their target. I say again do not be alarmed, I bear you no harm. My presence here today is aimed at achieving the exact opposite of harm; you will see that it is of extreme importance to you. Before I do make myself visible, I am afraid that I unavoidably have to resort to some actions that might appear to be magic, smoke and mirrors, trickery or showmanship. To the contrary, I am going to demonstrate technological capabilities that to you might appear to be impossible but are just pure physics applied differently relative to your present technologies. If you do gain some insight into the truth of what I am going to share with you today, then my display is worth my effort and the efforts of hundreds of species that I represent. I also profusely apologise to Newton and to Einstein by demonstrating that there are ways that the physical laws that they formulated and that all of you are used to, can be bent to suit special circumstances. I will now appear to you. I will materialise at an elevated spot in front of the podium to give you a chance to observe me. You will just be seeing advanced technology in action.' There was an incredulous babbling of voices and intakes of breath from the delegates at Rupert's statement and

181

then silence finally reigned again in the hall. With that Rupert uncloaked himself. A human-like form appeared.

Rupert appeared in front of the podium, floating upright in mid-air at a two-metre height above the floor. It looked like he was standing on an invisible pane of glass. He was dressed in a black tuxedo and looked very handsome using an athletic human form sporting greying hair. He looked just like any executive that would be found at a symposium on Earth. The builders monitoring the video feed from the UN were surprised to see Rupert's human form, having half expected him to make an appearance as a builder. What was obviously unusual to the front-row delegates in the hall is that they could look up to see the underside of Rupert's shoes. Rupert stayed in place but rotated himself slowly three times in a full circle so that everyone could take a look at his entire form while he rotated. There was another hub-hub of voices and disbelieving intakes of breath. Rupert waited again with raised arms until the furore had subsided. He was glad to see that although the ever-present security men were on full alert and moving closer, only a few of them had drawn their weapons. He smiled at them and held up his hands to show that he was not armed.

'I am a little thirsty after my trip so please excuse me if I take a sip of water.' With that Rupert floated down to the podium much to the surprise of the Secretary General and helped himself to some water from the jug and a handy glass. The builders were surprised to see Rupert drinking but realised it was for show and to placate the audience in the hall.

'Who are you and what do you want,' stammered the Secretary General.

'I originate from one of your ancestors, dating back hundreds of thousands of years. We seeded you on this planet about two million years ago. I am here to prevent this seeding becoming subject to another extinction. We are hoping that we can get you to all work together to counter a threat to your existence.'

Rupert glided back to his original point of appearance above the floor and faced the audience. Some security men ran to stand underneath Rupert but were obviously at a loss as to what to do with this floating person hovering above their heads.

'I presume that you can all see that I am not a hologram and that I can do what any one of you can do inclusive of partaking of some refreshment if I wish to do so. I feel that I need to further convince you that I have advanced technology at my disposal, so that you are more likely to listen to what I have to say. I have two other demonstrations that I prepared for you, both are innocuous and you need not be concerned. After the demonstrations I will explain why I am here today in detail and why the galactic federation decided to allow me to break a long-standing treaty that forbids the Federation to have any contact with Earth. As a first demonstration I wish to introduce you to a colleague of mine. She might look strange to you but her personality actually originates from a human on Earth.' With that a second form materialised above the podium, facing the audience alongside Rupert. Both forms looked as if they were standing side-by-side on the same invisible pane of glass that Rupert arrived on. The second form spoke.

'Hello delegates, how's it hanging?' asked Phydeau with a wicked glint in her red optics. This caused some disbelieving nervous laughter at several places in the hall.

'Look at that,' exclaimed a delegate. 'A speaking mechanical dog!'

'Who are you calling a mechanical dog you bag of bones,' growled the object of the demonstration and her tail was raised in the air like a scorpion's sting.

'Let me introduce you to Phydeau,' Rupert said. She helps to smooth over many a psychology-related problem for me and as such is a lot more than a mechanical dog. Her canine form is similar to the ones that many of you can relate to. You should be able to see that I have some involvement with human as well as mechanical sentient forms. She does tend to be sensitive as regards being called a mechanical dog as you have heard. You will all be able to interact with her some more in due course.' At this time, it became apparent that the newscasters in the room had their TV cameras fixed on the strange duo and were frantically recording the proceedings. Rupert stated that he had no objection to the recordings but that the news teams would find that they could not broadcast in any way or leave the hall due to a blanking field that was now in place for a limited time. He indicated that he needed to proceed with the second demonstration so he could start with the actual business that he had in mind. Until that was done, he did not wish to have the proceedings made public just yet. All cell phone communication was likewise blocked. Some delegates succumbed to panic and tried to leave the hall only to find that they could not penetrate the field. Rupert asked everyone to please be calm and to return to their seats.

He indicated that his second technology demonstration would now take place.

A large sturdy metallic table materialised on the floor in front of the podium. A large misshapen rock materialised beside Rupert and Phydeau about double the size of the candid canine. It floated away from the duo and came to rest on the table.

'As you can see, I have brought in a table and a solid untreated and unfinished granite rock weighing about a ton. I have also placed a chisel and a suitable hammer on the table. I need a volunteer from the audience please.' After some delay a delegate in the front row raised his hand. Rupert nodded his thanks and the man stepped closer to the table after identifying himself as Alan.

'Could you please use the hammer and the chisel and see if you can dent that rock,' Rupert requested Alan. Alan took the chisel and the hammer and enthusiastically began to pound away at the rock. After several minutes of pounding, that resulted in a few minuscule chips off the block of rock, Alan stepped back breathing heavily.

'OK, thank you; please take your seat.' Alan did so and the audience wondered what would happen next.

'I will now dress the rock for you,' Rupert said. With that the rock rose up from the table and moved over to be positioned in front of Rupert and Phydeau. The rock started to rotate in front of the duo and then suddenly it came apart. Six of its sides moved away from the rock's central core and then the detached pieces vanished, leaving behind a perfectly symmetrical cube. Smaller pieces left the cube's six sides and then also disappeared. The perfect cube moved back to the table and rested on the middle of it. Rupert asked Alan to investigate the cube and to tell the audience what he saw.

'I see a cube, all three of its dimensions seem to be identical at around one metre in length,' Alan said. 'The cube angles look like they are at exact right angles and the surface finish is perfectly smooth. I don't see any tool marks or vitrification. I have never seen anything like it before. There are identical inscriptions on all of the sides that I can see. The inscriptions consist of a circle enclosing the text "SS7".'

Rupert thanked Alan and Alan again returned to his seat.

'I used a Molecular Levitational Cutter, a MLC, that was specially pre-programmed for this demonstration. I hope that this cube will serve as my calling card and a pledge to you that we wish to help you to come of age as a seeding. If you do put bickering amongst yourselves behind you and you survive for a reasonable time into the future then maybe you could join the 1,376 other sentient species that are part of the galactic federation,' smiled Rupert.

'Incidentally, the MLC technology that you saw demonstrated today is how various seeding landing sites were built and civilisations were started on Earth. Puma Punku was built overnight by means of using teams of pre-programmed MLCs acting together, forming a modular building block conveyor system.'

Two chairs appeared next to the table facing the delegates and Rupert and Phydeau sat down in them. Phydeau's chair was specially adapted for her form and she looked perfectly comfortable. Alan piped up to ask what the 'SS7' stood for as inscribed inside the circles on the block of granite. Rupert answered to say that the peoples on Earth were the seventh sentient species that were seeded as originating from the

Pleiades constellation. That caused a further disbelieving babble of voices. Rupert waited patiently for the noise to subside, which it finally did. He went into some detail to describe the builder sentient species seeding initiatives that had taken place in the universe at different times.

'It is time for me to get to the actual reason for our visit today. I have a matter of extreme concern to share with you. We recently detected cloaked craft visiting Earth. The craft have been deploying swarms of transparent spheres at many points across the globe. These craft are not part of the galactic federation so we have concluded that Earth is being visited by a hostile sentient species seeking to seed itself on Earth, aiming at replacing the present SS7 human seeding. I have a video for you to provide you with the necessary evidence.' With that the video that Charles had recorded while testing his infrared long-distance sensors on planet 23 was played to the delegates. The long plume trailing behind the offending craft became visible. Rupert continued after explaining that there were enemies to the seeding process, these were called the dark teams. There were also unfriendly entities in the universe working with the dark teams. They camouflaged their space craft using cloaking technology. Rupert explained that the craft in the video was only visible by using infra-red detectors. He continued.

'We took samples of the plume that you saw trailing behind the craft and found that these spheres contain pathogens such as advanced and modified viruses aimed at destroying the entire ecology on Earth. Here are some of our testing results.' Rupert displayed Mavis' report results and it became obvious that a grim sentiment was settling over the audience. 'We have found that the speres have a timed-release function and also a self-destruct feature', said Rupert. 'We have cracked the self-destruct code so the good news is that the payload deployment codes have not yet been activated by the dark teams and we know how to neutralise the threat. The bad news is that we don't know when the dark teams intend to deploy the payloads so time is of the essence. We expect the attack to be launched within days or weeks at best. A further challenge is that the self-destruct sequence has to be transmitted to the codes from a transmitter that is within 100 metres from each sphere. The spheres have been deployed over large parts of Earth and the federation does not have sufficient craft or resources to neutralise the threat due to the large area that is involved. That is why I am here; we need you to help yourselves while the federation and its builders take action in parallel.'

A delegate asked, 'What is it that we need to do exactly?' Rupert answered by saying that the first step should be to inform the population that federation craft would begin to cross over Earth at low altitudes and that these craft were friendly, if they were seen. No anti-aircraft or air-to-air defences should be engaged against them. Social media should be blocked from distributing false information about what was shared today, as regards the enemy craft and its threat. Defence forces and commercial entities on Earth should deploy as many spere disrupters as possible as soon as possible, using ground and air resources.' Rupert was asked where the delegates could obtain sufficient quantities of sphere disrupters and if the neutralising actions would not alert the dark teams to the threat counter measures that were taking place, causing them to strike earlier.

'If you look to the back of the hall, you will find several boxes that contain millions of disruptors. The disruptors have been pre-programmed and only need to be switched on. I will see to it that several of our builders are made available to you for purposes of training and disruptor deployment. As regards alerting the dark teams, the federation is busy sending several motherships to Earth with a view to aiding in disrupter deployment and also to monitor and engage enemy forces if and when they are discovered. We anticipate that if there are sufficient combined actions between yourselves and the federation, then we will be able to negate this threat. If there are any further questions, I ask you to be patient and to address them to me or Phydeau one at a time. I am sure that the secretary general will be able to handle that protocol for us. If need be, I can bring additional builders into the hall to allow your questions to be answered as quickly as possible. We do suggest that all of you should engage in planning with your military and commercial resources in order to get disruptors available all over the globe as soon as possible. We are now going to remove the blanking field, to allow you to take action. We are also available for further questions.' With that there was a flurry of delegate indications of pending questions and the duo started handling them as fast as they could. Back in Persephone, the trainee builders realised that they would be needed to help deploy disrupters and perform some training actions. They waited for further instructions in that regard. While they waited Rupert and Phydeau continued answering a flurry of questions back at the UN hall.

Chapter Fifteen

(Where the New Alliance Takes Action)

'How do we know that you are not actually intending to invade Earth?' enquired a belligerent delegate.

'I was hoping that our demonstrations today made it abundantly clear that we have access to technologies that you have not yet mastered on Earth. If we wished to invade, we could have done so a long time ago. In actual fact you could be thought of as being our children. Parents mostly look after their children. The universe is huge. There are more than enough resources and opportunities for all seeded species.

Furthermore, we warned you about the pathogenic threat facing you. If we were happy to see the SS7 seeding ecology being destroyed in its entirety, all we needed to do, was to do nothing. We are here to help you and to counter the dark team and reptilian threat.' Rupert responded. There was an interruption from the other end of the table. Merriment erupted and everyone turned their gaze onto Phydeau. She was amusing a gaggle of lady delegates by coquettishly batting her false eyelashes. She had changed her garb to a scanty polka dot yellow bikini. It seemed that some measure of trust was being established between the audience and the builders, regardless of Phydeau's strange form. A question was fired at Phydeau.

'Where exactly have these spheres been deployed so we know where our forces need to focus their use of the disruptors?' asked a lady delegate.

'We have located several spots on Earth that have shown signs of contagion sphere presence. If you observe the screens here in the hall you will see a list of GPS coordinates and the equivalent name of the affected areas,' Phydeau growled. The delegates were dismayed to see that most of their countries featured on a long list. It appeared that the dark teams had been initiating their clandestine attack for some time. The question-and-answer session continued unabated.

'What assistance can we expect from the galactic federation?'

'As we speak several thousand federation craft are being prepared for transit to Earth. They will start to appear around this planet within hours. They will commence with grid immunisation pattern flights arranged at around 100 metres above the terrain in the infected areas. In the interim all delegates are urged to get their resources equipped with disruptors. You need to initiate your own grid immunisation patterns as soon as possible, the more the merrier. There is no need to see to federation craft airspace flight planning, all of our craft are fitted with automatic collision avoidance equipment and they can manoeuvre at greater speeds and accelerations than any of your UN aircraft,' stated Rupert.

'Are there any cloaked dark team craft anywhere in Earth's airspace right now?'

'That is an excellent question. We have deployed several sentient long-range surveillance aircraft to several locations on Earth. Our latest sensor suite is in action right now, managed by a builder named Charles and others like him with the mandate to search for cloaked craft. To give you an indication as to what is being monitored, I have now patched in a live video feed from Charles on one of the screens in this hall,' Rupert advised. With that a video feed from Charles was projected for the delegates. All of them watched the live video feed for a time with considerable interest.

'How did the federation come into being, was there an entity that initiated all creation? We are concerned about the possible effects on our population of revealing the existence of extra-terrestrial visitors to Earth. Some cultures believe in a solitary deity and that might impact upon their religious beliefs, leading to dismay. Chaos might erupt.'

Phydeau responded. 'We have taken note that some cultures on Earth believe in many deities and others believe in single deities or none at all. Our arrival should not make any difference since we know that there was a supreme builder. We know that the builder was very active in the seeding process aeons ago. Eventually, the supreme builder deployed, and was complemented by, many builder teams. The teams saw to the propagation of seedings across the galaxy under the supreme builder's direction. Some cultures on Earth that believed in groups of deities interacted with these builder teams. Other cultures interacted with solitary builders and that is why various religions and beliefs exist on Earth. Our visit should not deviate from the beliefs that exist. There might be slight differences to how cultures view religion and the associated beliefs, that should not detract from what is already in vogue on Earth.' There was a sudden commotion amongst the group of delegates monitoring

Charles's live video feed and everyone switched their attention to the video.

Charles had locked his auto tracker onto a peanut-shaped craft shown as a black object against a white background in the infrared video image. The object was obviously cloaked since Charles's attempts to provide a colour video image failed although his auto tracker stayed locked. It could be deduced from the video image that Charles was switching between various sensors that covered different parts of the electromagnetic spectrum. When his colour sensor was engaged, the peanut-shaped craft seemed to vanish. Suddenly three cigar-shaped craft also appeared in the infrared video image. Rupert spoke up and told the assembled delegates that these were Pleiades battle cruisers that had just arrived from the constellation's seven sister star cluster. While the delegates watched in awe, the battle cruisers each fired a salvo of missiles at the peanut-shaped intruder. The intruder had a dark plume exiting from the rear of the craft at that time. The missiles left a visible trail behind them as they accelerated towards the dark team craft. When they got close to the intruder there were violent flashes of white light as the missile payloads detonated. Charles's video display bloomed to a solid white as his sensor arrays overloaded. The audience in the UN hall exclaimed in awe. After several seconds the solid white video bloom subsided since Charles had engaged his image contrast filters. There was no longer any evidence of the dark team craft to be seen. The three friendly craft were however still in evidence. One Pleiades craft performed a 360-degree victory roll. It was obvious to the assembled delegates that when the friendly battle cruisers were viewed from above or underneath, that they were saucer shaped. Seen from the side the craft resembled cigars. The three craft accelerated away from the scene at speeds that no Earthly craft could match while the debris cloud left behind from the destruction of the intruder started to dissipate.

'Well delegates, there is some additional evidence for you that we are here to assist Earth in resisting its ecological extinction attack.' Rupert was interrupted at this point by a commotion amongst the delegates.

'My friend has vanished! He was standing right next to me a second ago,' exclaimed a lady in the audience. Rupert moved over to speak to her and while he did so, there were two other nearby delegates that exclaimed in the same manner, their colleagues had also suddenly vanished apparently into thin air.

'I have some further information to share with you. We now know that the dark team forces have infiltrated agents into Earth's society in order to assist in achieving their objective of destroying Earth's ecology. They wish to seed themselves here instead. These are shape shifters that camouflage themselves to look like humans but they are actually alien to SS7. Their disappearance means that we have to expedite our countermeasures. Their agents operate by spreading false information in clever ways so as to support their hidden agenda. They spread lies and garner unwitting human support such as warning people away from vaccination initiatives. That results in deaths and virus mutations that would otherwise have been avoided. Since three entities vanished from this hall at the instant that the dark team craft was destroyed, it is obvious that these were dark team agents that have retreated. Incidentally I have been informed that federation cruisers have destroyed another two dark team craft attempting to deploy more spheres while we were speaking,' said Rupert while the assembled delegates looked at each other disbelievingly. Several conversations blossomed. Rupert waited for the babble of voices to subside.

'We urgently need to get moving in order to prevent the dark team from triggering the spheres. Destroying three of their craft is a good start to stopping the spheres from being spread or activated but we need to destroy the spheres that have already been deployed. I need warn you that some other federation assets will be taking part in this clean-up process. I am doing so to prevent the situation where your defence forces start attacking what they might mistake as enemy dark teams. Friendly fire is not friendly! All federation forces will be cloaked while they perform the cleansing process so as not to cause panic amongst Earth's population but it is possible that observant humans might pick up that something is amiss. No doubt all of you delegates will let information slip either intentionally or unintentionally. It is suggested that all delegates should wait before spreading too much information in an uncoordinated manner. Everyone should work together on a media campaign to inform the peoples on Earth as to what has transpired today.' Rupert paused and then continued his narrative.

'As further evidence of our planned assistance to all of you, I wish to present four more builders to you. I need to show you what they look like and inform you as to what they will be doing in a bit more detail. These are builders that will immediately be engaged in using sphere disruptors to negate the threat around and within New York. Other similar builders will be assisting larger federation craft all around the planet. As before, please do not be alarmed since your newest visitors bear you no harm and as you now know, they are here to assist you. They will appear in this hall just like Phydeau and I did. They will uncloak in the same spot where we did.' With that everyone in the hall peered up at the now familiar area above the floor where the presentation to the UN delegates had begun earlier that day.

A quartet of builders appeared, this time the audience in the hall was more prepared for their sudden arrival but they still did exclaim at viewing the visitors for the first time. Four robot-like entities appearing before one can be quite daunting, whether they were friendly or not. All four appeared to be dressed in what resembled painted-on suits. Subtle differences identified female versus male traits. Rupert introduced Hermien, Mavis, Peter and Chris. He informed the assembly that this quartet had been instrumental in helping to detect and analyse the substance of the dark team attack. They had also just been tasked by the federation council to assist in negating the threat to Earth. The quartet chorused a greeting that was echoed by some delegates disbelievingly, the audience started to realise that these entities were sentient and capable of independent thought and action. Rupert explained that Chris and Peter were an engineering team and that they had eavesdropped on dark team representatives infiltrated into the World Economic Forum at Davos. The intent to decrease Earth's human population and to destroy Earth's entire ecology had been discovered at that time. Hermien and Mavis were introduced as a biological support team that had obtained sphere samples and had quantified the threat posed by the spheres. Rupert moved on to describe some of the builder attributes.

'These builders do not have any need for a craft to transport them. They can teleport to where they wish to be and that means they can actually transit between any planets in our universe in a rapid manner. They are capable of moving at speeds and enduring accelerations that would turn human flesh into jelly. Their prime function at this time is actually to support federation seeding initiatives. Specifically, their job is to ensure seeding long-term survival. They are presently engaged in testing seeding SS23. This latest seeding is located about ten light years from here. However, this team has been temporarily tasked along with several others of their build standard to defend Earth against the SS7 attack. They are fully sentient just like any one of you. Indeed, all four of them used to live on Earth.' This latest revelation left most delegates in a state of confusion and shock. Rupert continued.

'I know that you all have many questions that you wish to have answered. I will now encourage you to speak with these builders. I wish to locate them to a more comfortable location for you to do so. Please move away from the table where Phydeau and I are sitting. I will bring in another table and several chairs.' After the delegates had made a suitable space, Rupert teleported in another table and eight chairs. Four chairs were comfortably padded, definitely more suited to human occupants. The other four chairs were suited to the constraints imposed upon the builder forms such as their size and mass. Chris, Peter, Mavis and Hermien sank down into their chairs next to Phydeau and Rupert, facing the audience. The other four chairs were arranged diametrically opposite to the builders on the other side of the table. Rupert invited delegates to take one of the four seats and after some hesitation four delegates sat down and inspected each of the builders in front of them with trepidation. Groups of standing delegates formed behind the tables and mostly listened attentively to what was being said. Another flurry of questions began.

A delegate wanted to know if it was possible to obtain access to federation technology such as the molecular levitational cutter. Rupert responded by saying that history had shown that if technology was made available too early to a sentient species that had not matured sufficiently to adopt respect and tolerance of the general society, genocide could be triggered. The seeding on the entire planet could self-destruct. However, SS7 was being re-evaluated for its maturity readiness by the galactic council and might be allowed to apply for federation membership in due course, now that the existence of the federation was known to Earth. Certainly, MLC and other technology could speed up productivity and help to reduce carbon emissions. Global warming and air pollution effects were known to reduce seeding long-term survival and were becoming urgent problems for receiving attention on Earth.

The quartet's origins were probed at length and each builder presented a summary of his and her history while avoiding specifics such as their names while they were on Earth and how they were chosen to be builders. The quartet had obviously been briefed not to reveal certain matters to humans, so as to avoid paranoia and fear. Questions relating to builder inbuilt equipment were also fielded without providing any specifics. Rupert interrupted the flurry of questions at that point to say that new video material was available and that delegates should again look at the various screens in the hall.

'I have projected several views of Earth for you to view in real time, at different locations and at different heights above ground. Those of you that are used to Google Earth[ddd] will recognise your own satellite images. We have superimposed a red overlay across all of the world areas to indicate where the pathogenic spheres have been deployed. Green areas on the overlay indicate where some affected areas have already been subjected to sphere disruptor cleansing,' Rupert explained.

The delegates inspected the video images, noted the large red expanses and the relatively small green areas on the displays. Concern was evident on many faces. New York was predominantly red and that included the area around the UN headquarters. While the delegates watched, they could see some red areas elsewhere slowly tuning to green. Rupert made a further announcement.

'I need you to please excuse the four of our builders that you have been interacting with for the past hour. I will remain here with Phydeau to address any further concerns that you may have, to coordinate activities as they occur in real time and to share progress with all of you. Our builder team will now cloak and move outside this building to commence with the local sphere clean-up activities. You will be able to monitor their progress in real time on the screens in front of you. I am able to report that we now have over five hundred federation resources that have been mobilised to neutralise the

---

[ddd] Google Earth is a computer program that features stitched-together satellite views of the Earth's (and other planet) features in a layered manner, at different resolutions. Zooming into and out of places anywhere on Earth is possible.

spheres.' With that the builder quartet vanished from the room and all delegates' attentions became focused on the New York and other aerial displays. The audience noted that the area around the headquarters and elsewhere had started to turn to green away from the unwanted red on the video displays and a relieved cheer went up. At that time the secretary general declared the introduction part of the presentation to be closed. He indicated that he wished to further interact with the remaining two builders in the hall but that other delegates were welcome to monitor the proceedings. Delegates started to drift out of the hall in dribs and drabs, with several of the remaining delegates talking animatedly on their cell phones and taking picture of the builders, their granite block calling card and the various video images arranged around the hall. The hall's video images were slowly but surely changing from red to green. Everyone realised that the hall had effectively been transformed into a joint operations centre. The secretary general had food and drinks brought into the hall and invited Rupert and Phydeau to partake of some nourishment. He wasn't too surprised when they informed him that they did not need any food. Eating was sometimes performed just for show. The food was always subsequently disposed of. The secretary and remaining delegates chose to eat what they wished. It wasn't too long before senior military commanders started to arrive in the hall along with their supporting staff and security staff. Rupert continued to placate groups of arrivals and ensured them that everyone was perfectly safe.

Suddenly, Phydeau sprang from her chair and flew across the room over the heads of all bystanders, to knock over a security guard that had drawn his pistol. He ended up lying on his back on the floor. The guard managed to retain his pistol and fired two shots at Phydeau that had no effect. Several delegates screamed in shock at the unbelievable scene unfolding before them. There was a crunching sound as titanium-tipped canines clamped down on the guard's upper thigh as Phydeau retaliated. He fired another two shots at her head and she shifted her grip to his throat in one fluid motion. Another crunching sound was followed by some gurgling and the guard ceased to move; his pistol dropped to the ground. A second guard ran towards the podium and pointed his pistol at Rupert's head. Two shots rang out.

The second assassin stiffened and then fell down onto the floor. A third security guard that had been standing at the podium hovering behind the secretary general slowly lowered his weapon and holstered it. Rupert nodded to the guard and then moved over to the now prone attacker's form on the floor with its two gunshot wounds to the head. While the onlookers studied the prone form on the floor, the body slowly started to change its shape. The body took on a scaly appearance and changed in colour from normal human tones to various shades of green. The fluid leaking from the corpse was seen to not be red but was an oily green instead. Rupert spoke.

'Ah, I see we have a reptilian class shape shifter sentient species with us today. They are obviously behind the dark team attack on Earth. Their attempt to assassinate me was obviously driven by a need for revenge after we destroyed three of their craft. They wanted to slow down our sphere disruption initiative to give them more time to trigger contagion. I don't recognise this particular species. That confirms they are not signatories to the galactic federation. We do have some colleagues from the Orion Constellation on a craft circling Earth. I will teleport these two attackers to that craft for analysis by our onboard Orion reptilian seeding colleagues. Then we will see if we will gain further intelligence and allow us to construct shape shifter detection devices.' With that the two bodies vanished from the hall. The delegates noted that the green sticky mess that had been spreading from the two forms had also vanished, leaving a pristine floor behind. A cacophony of voices again broke out and Rupert waited until the burbling subsided sufficiently such that he could be heard.

'Phydeau my friend, I must congratulate you on detecting that threat so quickly and for taking the action that you did. You are really good at sniffing out threats! It is true that I am protected by a surrounding stasis field but it is still unpleasant to be hit by high energy metallic projectiles. I further have a special word of thanks to the secretary general's security guard that dispatched the second reptilian assassin so ably. If it is possible for all of us to support each other in this manner as reflected by today's happenings, then that bodes great things for the future of humanity and their possible future inclusion in the galactic federation,' smiled Rupert. Phydeau rolled her red optics and opened her fang-stained jaws.

'I keep telling everyone that I am not just a pretty face. I guess I went beyond my normal mandate a bit today, to shift towards being a bodyguard. I must say that the dark team reptilians don't taste very nice at all. I prefer kissing frogs to biting them,' smiled Phydeau with a humorous glint in her red optics. Rupert decided that it was time to bring the joint planning session to order. Many introductions took place between the duo and a multitude of military advisors and diplomatic staff. All of the senior delegates inspected the stone block on the table and the displays around the hall in wonder. Rupert spoke and received a nod of agreement from the secretary general.

'Gentlemen and ladies, if you take a look at the displays around this hall and note the small percentage of green on the overlay in comparison to the red, you will realise that we have a lot of work to do.' With that some vestige of order descended upon the crowd and the detailed coordination of Earth's forces along with those from the galactic federation kicked off in earnest.

Chapter Sixteen

(Where the Quartet Returns to Active Duty)

'Congratulations on successfully taking part in negating the threat to Earth! In the process you have possibly managed to get SS7 accepted again for galactic council evaluation. That might lead to possible membership of the galactic federation,' Olympus smiled.

'The good news is that our sensors indicate that all of the pathogenic spheres have been destroyed. We have also heard from our Orion colleagues. They have been able to devise shape shifter detectors. The detectors allow shape shifter detection even when the shifters have shifted to emulate a different seeded species. Sufficient quantities of the detectors have been provided to SS7. They are busy installing them at key locations around Earth. Our new friends on Earth have noticed that some of their previous colleagues have recently suddenly vanished from many Earth locations. We can conclude that the enemy is leaving the planet and hopefully abandoning their plan to destroy Earth's ecology. The destruction of the ecology was intended to be followed by their occupation of planet seven. Interestingly there has also been a dramatic reduction in social media false news on Earth.

Obviously, the dark team media disinformation campaign has been dealt a severe blow. Lies about topics such as the dangers of vaccinations and that global warming is not an issue to be concerned about have somewhat abated. Some federation resources have been tasked with monitoring Earth and its environs for a time to prevent a recurrence of the dark team attack. Unfortunately, that means Charles will only be visiting SSTEP for times when we specifically need his services for performing SS23 field testing.

'Negotiations have commenced between the federation and the SS7 United Nations, led by Rupert, as to the conditions for any technology transfer to Earth. Included in the discussions are the prerequisites for galactic federation membership. It is really hoped that the peoples on Earth can put aside their petty differences. They need to abandon senseless wars such that they can clean up not only their act but also their planet. The federation has already invested a lot of time and resources in the SS7 seeding and it is time for them to be more appreciative of what they have been given. Time will tell. In the meantime, our prime task must continue. You no longer require my assistance to integrate with SSTEP policies, actions and procedures. I am releasing all four of you to your mentors for active duty. Your mentors will handle your daily tasks from now on. You can always contact me if you encounter any problems that you feel you cannot handle. I have noted that the four of you have formed a strong bond. I can tell that you intend to support each other whenever necessary. I am sure that Hermien and Chris will continue to support each other as will Peter and Mavis. I understand that you like playing bridge and there are other SSTEP pursuits that you are aware of. On top of that, as I am sure you know,

Phydeau is always available to you.' The canny canine suddenly appeared before them, he/she must have been eavesdropping. She waved a taloned paw in farewell with her red optics reflecting a slightly saddened glint at the changed circumstances. Four builder mentors then appeared in the room and Chris was pleased to see that Brian was once again there to mentor him. The four builders with their mentors retired to various cubicles after a vote of thanks to Olympus and Rupert. Olympus cheerfully waved them on and he departed from Persephone. The newest builders at SSTEP did the same, in anticipation of the briefing by their mentors.

'You can't complain about your eventful life, can you?' enquired Brian of Chris.

'No, you are right,' admitted Chris. He indicated that he had been wondering what Brian had been doing while the four recruits had been on special assignment on Earth.

'I was preparing for the next intake of recruits,' Brian said. 'I have to make sure that there are sufficient mechanical shells in a suitably tested state for the recordings to be transferred to, that the trainees have cubicles at their disposal and that their training and induction plan is in place,' explained Brian. Chris asked if he could ask a personal question and Brian told him to go ahead. Chris asked what job Brian had on Earth when he was still alive and how he had transitioned to SSTEP.

'I was a technical training facility manager at an educational institute during my entire professional career,' Brian confided. 'I retired to live next to the South African coast, I always enjoyed fishing. I unfortunately suffered a heart attack while I was taking a swim in the sea and my body washed up on the beach some days after that. My wife was greatly saddened and lonely after that. I was just as surprised as you were when I found myself in a new form here at SSTEP. That was many years ago. I progressed from a trainee to a senior builder here at SSTEP. I have mentored several builders since then, I have lost count of the number. OK Chris, it is time to discuss what is expected of you as regards your SS23 assignment. You will be working with Hermien and Mavis on a daily basis for some time. Peter has been temporarily assigned to manage another one of SSTEPs programs. The three of you will be investigating the SS23 seeding newly designed capabilities. The brain capacity upgrade in comparison to SS7, as well as changes to DNA robustness and the endocrine system enhancements need to be evaluated and laboratory tested. You will investigate the long-term SS23 build standard robustness using computer modelling, simulation and sub-system trials. The SS23 build standard changes are aimed at reducing the incidence of unwanted DNA mutations that lead to birth deformities. There is a need to reduce stroke severity by the addition of redundant brain capacity. Heart backup upgrades will be investigated with a view to reducing heart attack probabilities. You will primarily be assigned to the integration laboratory where you will specifically address the SS23 basic programming. In particular you will be stationed at the brain and heart integration benches. Microbiological evaluations will need to take place to ensure that the envisaged DNA upgrades have a reduced incidence of cancer formation and a reduction in the negative gene transmissions between seedling generations.

You will need to perform billions of Monte Carlo [eee] simulations to determine the impacts of the enhanced SS23 genome relative to SS7. A recent addition to the new build standard is the inclusion of nanites to the seedling's defence system. You will test to confirm if that design addition supplements the seedling's defences against pathogens and viral attacks. Do you have any questions?' enquired Brian. Chris did not, he was feeling exhilarated at finally doing something that he was commissioned to do.

Brian greeted Chris and left Chris' cubicle. Chris did likewise, he teleported to the door in the SSTEP corridor entitled 'Integration Laboratory SS23'. Mentally taking a deep breath, the builder entered the laboratory.

To be continued...

[eee] Monte Carlo simulations are performed by varying inputs to a process and evaluating the results of the input parameter changes. The technique is often used to test the robustness of a process.